WINNIPEG
WITHDRAWN
DEC 0 9 2010
PUBLIC LIBRARY

D0820262

The Girl Who Chased the Moon

**Center Point
Large Print**

Also by Sarah Addison Allen
and available from Center Point Large Print:

The Sugar Queen

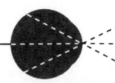

**This Large Print Book carries the
Seal of Approval of N.A.V.H.**

The Girl Who Chased the Moon

Sarah Addison Allen

CENTER POINT PUBLISHING
THORNDIKE, MAINE

This Center Point Large Print edition is published in
the year 2010 by arrangement with Bantam Books,
an imprint of The Random House Publishing Group,
a division of Random House, Inc.

Copyright © 2010 by Sarah Addison Allen.

All rights reserved.

The Girl Who Chased the Moon is a work of fiction.
Names, characters, places, and incidents either are the
product of the author's imagination or are used
fictitiously. Any resemblance to actual persons, living or
dead, events, or locales is entirely coincidental.

The text of this Large Print edition is unabridged.
In other aspects, this book may vary
from the original edition.
Printed in the United States of America
on permanent paper.
Set in 16-point Times New Roman type.

ISBN: 978-1-60285-833-6

Library of Congress Cataloging-in-Publication Data

Allen, Sarah Addison.
 The girl who chased the moon / Sarah Addison Allen.
   p. cm.
 ISBN 978-1-60285-833-6 (library binding : alk. paper)
 1. Family secrets—Fiction. 2. North Carolina—Fiction. 3. Large type books. I. Title.
 PS3601.L4356G57 2010b
 813'.6—dc22

                                                              2010010042

To the memory of famous gentle giant
Robert Pershing Wadlow (1918–1940).
At the time of his death at age twenty-two,
he was eight feet eleven inches tall—
a world record that has never been broken.

Chapter 1

It took a moment for Emily to realize the car had come to a stop. She looked up from her charm bracelet, which she'd been worrying in slow circles around her wrist, and stared out the window. The two giant oaks in the front yard looked like flustered ladies caught mid-curtsy, their starched green leaf-dresses swaying in the wind.

"This is it?" she asked the taxi driver.

"Six Shelby Road. Mullaby. This is it."

Emily hesitated, then paid him and got out. The air outside was tomato-sweet and hickory-smoked, all at once delicious and strange. It automatically made her touch her tongue to her lips. It was dusk, but the streetlights weren't on yet. She was taken aback by how quiet everything was. It suddenly made her head feel light. No street sounds. No kids playing. No music or television. There was this sensation of otherworldliness, like she'd traveled some impossible distance.

She looked around the neighborhood while the taxi driver took her two overstuffed duffel bags out of the trunk. The street consisted of large old homes, most of which were showpieces in true old-movie Southern fashion with their elaborate trim work and painted porches.

The driver set her bags on the sidewalk beside

her, nodded, then got behind the wheel and drove off.

Emily watched him disappear. She tucked back some hair that had fallen out of her short ponytail, then grabbed the handles of the duffel bags. She dragged them behind her as she followed the walkway from the sidewalk, through the yard and under the canopy of fat trees. It grew dark and cold under the trees, so she picked up her pace. But when she emerged from under the canopy on the other side, she stopped short at the sight before her.

The house looked nothing like the rest of the houses in the neighborhood.

It had probably been an opulent white at one time, but now it was gray, and its Gothic Revival pointed-arch windows were dusty and opaque. It was outrageously flaunting its age, spitting paint chips and old roofing shingles into the yard. There was a large wraparound porch on the first floor, the roof of which served as a balcony for the second floor, and years of crumbling oak leaves were covering both. If not for the single clear path formed by use up the center of the steps, it would have looked like no one lived there.

This was where her mother grew up?

She could feel her arms trembling, which she told herself was from the weight of the bags. She walked up the steps to the porch, dragging the duffel bags and a good many leaves with her. She set the bags down and walked to the door, then knocked once.

No answer.

She tried again.

Nothing.

She tucked her hair back again, then looked behind her as if to find an answer. She turned back and opened the rusty screen door and called into the house, "Hello?" The space sounded hollow.

No answer.

She entered cautiously. No lights were on, but the last sunlight of the day was coughing through the dining room windows, directly to her left. The dining room furniture was dark and rich and ornate, but it seemed incredibly large to her, as if made for a giant. To her right was obviously another room, but there was an accordion door closing off the archway. Straight in front of her was a hallway leading to the kitchen and a wide staircase leading to the second story. She went to the base of the stairs and called up, "Hello?"

At that moment, the accordion door flew open and Emily jumped back. An elderly man with coin-silver hair walked out, ducking under the archway to avoid hitting his head. He was fantastically tall and walked with a rigid gait, his legs like stilts. He seemed badly constructed, like a skyscraper made of soft wood instead of concrete. He looked like he could splinter at any moment.

"You're finally here. I was getting worried." His

fluid Southern voice was what she remembered from their first and only phone conversation a week ago, but he was nothing like she expected.

She craned her neck back to look up at him. "Vance Shelby?"

He nodded. He seemed afraid of her. It flustered her that someone this tall would be afraid of anything, and she suddenly found herself monitoring her movements, not wanting to do anything to startle him.

She slowly held out her hand. "Hi, I'm Emily."

He smiled. Then his smile turned into a laugh, which was an ashy roar, like a large fire. Her hand completely disappeared in his when he shook it. "I know who you are, child. You look just like your mother when she was your age." His smile faded as quickly as it had appeared. He dropped his hand, then looked around awkwardly. "Where are your suitcases?"

"I left them on the porch."

There was a short silence. Neither of them had known the other existed until recently. How could they have run out of things to say already? There was so much she wanted to know. "Well," he finally said, "you can do what you want upstairs— it's all yours. I can't get up there anymore. Arthritis in my hips and knees. This is my room now." He pointed to the accordion door. "You can choose any room you want, but your mother's old room was the last one on the right. Tell me what the wallpaper looks like when you walk in. I'd like to know."

"Thank you. I will," she said as he turned and walked away from her, toward the kitchen, his steps loud in his wondrously large shoes.

Emily watched him go, confused. That was it?

She went to the porch and dragged her bags in. Upstairs, she found a long hallway that smelled woolly and tight. There were six doors. She walked down the hall, the scraping of her duffel bags magnified in the hardwood silence.

Once she reached the last door on the right, she dropped her duffel bags and reached to the inside wall for the light switch. The first thing she noticed when the light popped on was that the wallpaper had rows and rows of tiny lilacs on it, like scratch-and-sniff paper, and the room actually smelled a little like lilacs. There was a four-poster bed against the wall, the torn, gauzy remnants of what had once been a canopy now hanging off the posts like maypoles.

There was a white trunk at the foot of the bed. The name *Dulcie,* Emily's mother's name, was carved in it in swirly letters. As she walked by it, she ran her hand over the top of the trunk and her fingertips came away with puffs of dust. Underneath the age, like looking though a layer of ice, there was a distinct impression of privilege to this room.

It made no sense. This room looked nothing like her mother.

She opened the set of French doors and stepped out onto the balcony, crunching into dried oak leaves that were ankle-deep. Everything had felt so precarious since her mother's death, like she was walking on a bridge made of paper. When she'd left Boston, it had been with a sense of hope, like coming here was going to make everything okay. She'd actually been comforted by the thought of falling back into a cradle of her mother's youth, of bonding with the grandfather she hadn't known she had.

Instead, the lonely strangeness of this place mocked her.

This didn't feel like home.

She reached to touch her charm bracelet for comfort, but felt only bare skin. She lifted her wrist, startled.

The bracelet was gone.

She looked down, then around. She frantically kicked the leaves on the balcony, trying to find it. She rushed back into the room and dragged her bags in, thinking maybe the bracelet had caught on one of them and slipped inside. She tossed her clothes out of them and accidentally dropped her laptop, which she'd wrapped in her white winter coat.

But it wasn't anywhere. She ran out of the room and down the stairs, then she banged out of the front door. It was so dark under the canopy of trees now that she had to slow down until the light from the streetlights penetrated, then she ran to the side-walk.

After ten minutes of searching, she realized that either she had dropped it on the sidewalk and someone had already taken it, or it had fallen out in the cab when she was toying with it and it was now on its way back to Raleigh—where the cab had picked her up at the bus station.

The bracelet had belonged to her mother. Dulcie had loved it—loved the crescent moon charm in particular. That charm had been worn thin by the many times Dulcie had rubbed it while in one of her faraway moods.

Emily walked slowly back into the house. She couldn't believe she'd lost it.

She heard what sounded like a clothes dryer door slam, then her grandfather came out of the kitchen. "Lilacs," she said when he met her in the foyer, where she had stopped and waited for him to notice her so she wouldn't startle him. How odd that he was the giant, yet she was the one who felt out of place.

He gave her a cautious look, like she was out to trick him. "Lilacs?"

"You asked what the wallpaper was in Mom's old room. It's lilacs."

"Ah. It was always flowers, usually roses, when she was a little girl. It changed a lot as she got older. I remember once it was lightning bolts on a tar-black background. And then another time it was this scaly blue color, like a dragon's belly. She hated that one, but couldn't seem to change it."

That made Emily smile. "That doesn't sound like her at all. I remember once . . ." She stopped when Vance looked away. He didn't want to know. The last time he saw his daughter was twenty years ago. Wasn't he even curious? Stung, Emily turned away from him. "I guess I'll go to bed now."

"Are you hungry?" he asked as he followed her at a distance. "I went to the grocery store this morning. I bought some teenager food."

She reached the first step on the staircase and turned, which made him step back suddenly. "Thank you. But I really am tired."

He nodded. "All right. Tomorrow, maybe."

She went back to the bedroom and fell onto the bed. Mustiness exploded from the mattress. She stared at the ceiling. Moths had come in, attracted to the light, and they were hopping around the cob-webby chandelier. Her mother had grown up with a *chandelier* in her bedroom? This from the same woman who would lecture Emily if she left a light on in a room she wasn't using.

She reached over and pulled some of her clothes from the floor and buried her face in them. They smelled familiar, like her mother's incense. She squeezed her eyes shut, trying not to cry. It was too early to say this was a bad decision. And even if it was, there was nothing she could do about it. She could survive a year here, surely.

She heard the wind skittering dried leaves around the balcony, something she realized sounded remarkably like someone walking around out there. She moved the clothes from her face and turned her head to look out the open balcony doors.

The light from the bedroom illuminated the closest treetops in the backyard, but their limbs weren't swaying. She sat up and crawled off the bed. Once outside, she looked around carefully. "Is anyone here?" she called, not knowing what she would do if someone actually answered.

Something suddenly caught her eye. She quickly stepped to the balustrade. She thought she saw something in the woodline beyond the gazebo in the overgrown backyard.

There! There it was again. It was a bright white light—a quick, zippy flash—darting between the trees. Gradually, the light faded, moving back into the darkness of the woods until it disappeared completely.

Welcome to Mullaby, North Carolina, she thought. Home of ghost lights, giants, and jewelry thieves.

She turned to go back in and froze.

There, on the old metal patio table, sitting on top of a layer of dried leaves, was her mother's charm bracelet.

Where it hadn't been just minutes ago.

TOO MUCH wine.

That's what Julia would blame it on.

When she saw Stella in the morning, she would say, "Oh, and that thing I said about Sawyer last night, forget it. It was just the wine talking."

As Julia made her way up to her apartment that evening, she felt vaguely panicked and not at all mellow—as summer wine on the back porch with Stella usually made her. She only had six months before she was free of this town again, six months that were supposed to be easy, the downhill slope of her two-year plan. But with one tiny slip of the tongue, she'd just made things infinitely harder on herself. If what she said got back to Sawyer, he wouldn't let it rest. She knew him too well.

She opened the door at the top of the staircase and stepped into the narrow hallway. Nothing had been done to the upper story of Stella's house to make it look like an apartment. There were four doors off the hallway. One led to the bathroom, one to Julia's bedroom, one to a second bedroom that had been converted into a kitchen, and another to a tiny third bedroom that Julia used as a living room.

Years ago, after Stella's ex-husband had spent his way through Stella's trust fund, he'd decided they should bring in renters for extra money, so he'd put a long curtain at the top of the staircase and said, "Voilà! Instant apartment." Then he'd been surprised when there were no takers. Men of thoughtless actions are always surprised by consequences, Stella always said. The last year of his and Stella's marriage, he'd started leaving a fine black dust on everything he'd touched, proof of his black heart, Stella claimed. When she'd discovered the black dust on other women—sprinkled on the backs of their calves when they wore shorts on summer days, and behind their ears when they wore their hair up—Stella had finally kicked him out. Afterward she got her brother to put a door at the top of the staircase, and a sink and an oven hookup in one of the bedrooms, hoping something good might come from finishing something her lousy ex-husband had started. Julia was her first tenant.

Initially, Julia had been uneasy about renting a place from one of her old high school enemies. But she'd had no choice. Stella's apartment had been the only place Julia could afford when she'd moved back to Mullaby. She'd been surprised to find that despite their pasts, she and Stella actually got along. It was an unlikely friendship, one Julia still didn't know how to explain. Stella had been one of the most popular girls at Mullaby High, a member of Sassafras—what the elite group of pretty, sparkly girls had called themselves. Julia had been the girl everyone avoided in the hallways. She'd been sullen and rude and undeniably strange. She'd dyed her hair bright pink, worn a studded leather choker every day, and used eyeliner so thick and black that she'd looked bruised.

And her father had tried so hard not to notice.

Julia walked down the hall to her bedroom. But

before she turned on the light, she noticed a light coming from Vance Shelby's house next door. She went to her open window in the darkness and looked out. All the time she'd lived in Stella's house, all the sleepless nights she'd spent staring out this window, and she'd never once seen a light in the upstairs bedrooms next door. There was a teenager on the balcony. She was just standing there, as still as snow, staring into the woods behind Vance's house. She was willow-branch thin, had a cap of yellow hair, and a sad sort of vulnerability was wafting from her, making the night smell like maple syrup. There was something familiar about her, and that's when Julia suddenly remembered. Vance's granddaughter was coming to live with him. This past week at Julia's restaurant, it was all anyone could talk about. Some people were curious, some were fearful, and some were outright mean. Not everyone had forgiven this girl's mother for what she'd done.

Julia didn't like the thought of what the girl was in for. It made her feel stiff and anxious. Living down your own past was hard enough. You shouldn't have to live down someone else's.

Tomorrow morning, Julia decided, she'd make an extra cake at the restaurant to take to her.

Julia undressed and got in bed. Eventually the light went off next door. She sighed and turned on her side and waited to cross another day off her calendar.

• • •

AFTER HER father's death almost two years ago, Julia had taken a few days off work to come back to Mullaby to get his affairs in order. Her plan had been to quickly sell his house and restaurant, then take the money and go back to Maryland and finally make her dream of opening her own bakery come true.

But things hadn't gone exactly the way they were supposed to.

She'd quickly discovered that her father had been deeply in debt, his house and restaurant mortgaged to the hilt. Selling his house had paid off his home mortgage and a small part of his restaurant mortgage. But even with that, she would have barely broken even if she'd sold the restaurant then. So she came up with her now-infamous two-year plan. By living very frugally and bringing in more business to J's Barbecue while she was there, in two years she would have the mortgage paid off and could sell the restaurant for a tidy profit. She'd been perfectly up-front about it with everyone in town. She would be staying in Mullaby for two years, but that *did not mean she lived here anymore*. She was just visiting. That was all.

When she took over the restaurant, J's Barbecue had a modest but loyal following, thanks to her father. He had a way of making people feel happy when they left, smelling of sweet yellow barbecue smoke that trailed behind them like a dress train. But Mullaby had more barbecue restaurants per capita than any other place in the state, so competition was fierce. With her father's personal touch now gone, Julia knew the restaurant needed something to set it apart from the rest. So she started baking and selling cakes—her specialty—and it was an instant boon to business. Soon, J's Barbecue was known not just for fine Lexington-style barbecue, but also for the best cakes and pastries around.

Julia always got to the restaurant well before dawn, and the only person there before her was the pit cook. They rarely talked. He had his job and she had hers. She left the day-to-day running of the place to the people her father had taught and trusted. Even though the barbecue business was in her bones, stuck there like spurs, she tried to stay as uninvolved as possible. She loved her father, but it had been a long time since she'd wanted to be like him. When Julia was a child, before she'd turned into a moody, pink-haired teenager, she used to follow him to work every day before school and gladly help with everything from waitressing to tossing wood into the smokehouse pit. Some of her best memories were of spending time with her father at J's Barbecue. But too much had happened since then for her to ever believe she could be that comfortable here again. So she came in early, baked that day's cakes, and left just as the first early-bird customers arrived for breakfast. On good days, she didn't even see Sawyer.

This, as it turned out, wasn't a good day.

"You'll never guess what Stella told me last night," Sawyer Alexander said, strolling into the kitchen just as Julia was finishing the apple stack cake she was going to take to Vance Shelby's granddaughter.

Julia closed her eyes for a moment. Stella must have called him the moment Julia left her last night and went upstairs.

Sawyer stopped next to her at the stainless steel table and stood close. He was like crisp, fresh air. He was self-possessed and proud, but everyone forgave him for that because charm sparkled around him like sunlight. Blue-eyed and blond-haired, he was handsome, smart, rich, and fun to be around. And he was disgustingly kind, too, as all the men in his family were, filled to capacity with Southern gentility. Sawyer drove his grandfather to Julia's restaurant every morning just so he could have breakfast with his old cronies.

"You're not supposed to be back here," she said as she put the last layer of cake on top of the dried-apple and spice filling.

"Report me to the owner." He pushed some of her hair behind her left ear, his fingers lingering on the thin pink streak she still dyed in her hair there. "Don't you want to know what Stella told me last night?" he asked.

She jerked her head away from his hand as she put the last of the apple and spice filling on top of the cake, leaving the sides bare. "Stella was drunk last night."

"She said you told her that you bake cakes because of *me*."

Julia knew it was coming, but she stilled anyway, the icing spatula stopping mid-stroke. She quickly resumed spreading the filling, hoping he hadn't noticed. "She thinks you have low self-esteem. She's trying to build up your ego."

He lifted one eyebrow in that insolent way of his. "I've been accused of many things, but low self-esteem is not one of them."

"It must be hard to be so beautiful."

"It's hell. Did you really say that to her?"

She clanged the spatula into the empty bowl the filling had been in, then she took both to the sink. "I don't remember. I was drunk, too."

"You never get drunk," he said.

"You don't know me well enough to make blanket statements like 'You never get drunk.'" It felt good to say that. Eighteen years she'd been away. *Look how much I've improved,* she wanted to say.

"Fair enough. But I do know Stella. Even when she drinks, I've never known her to lie. Why would she tell me that you bake cakes because of me if it wasn't true?"

"I bake cakes. You have an infamous sweet tooth. Maybe she got the two tangled up." She walked into the storage room for a cake box, taking longer than necessary, hoping maybe he'd give up and go away.

"You're taking a cake with you?" he asked when she came back out. He hadn't moved. All the crazy-hot activity in the kitchen—waitresses going in and out, cooks going back and forth, the constant thump of barbecue being hand-chopped— and he was so still. She had to quickly turn away. Staring at an Alexander man too long was like staring at the sun. The image became imprinted. You could close your eyes and still see him.

"I'm giving it to Vance Shelby's granddaughter. She got in last night."

That made him laugh. "*You're* actually giving someone a *welcome* cake?"

She didn't realize the irony until he pointed it out to her. "I don't know what came over me."

He watched her as she put the cake in the cardboard box. "I like this color on you," he said, touching the sleeve of her white long-sleeved shirt.

She immediately pulled her arm away. A year and a half of avoiding this man since she'd been back, then she had to go and say to Stella the one thing that would draw him to her like gravity. He'd been looking for this excuse since the moment she came back to town. He wanted to get closer to her. She knew that. And it made her angry. How could he even *think* of picking up where they left off after what happened?

She reached over and closed the window above her table. It was always the last thing she did every morning, and sometimes it made her sad. Another day, another call unanswered. She picked up the cake box and took it with her out into the restaurant without another word to Sawyer.

J's Barbecue was plain, as most genuine barbecue restaurants in the South were—linoleum floors, plastic tablecloths on the tables, heavy wooden booths. It was an homage to tradition. As soon as she'd taken over, Julia had pulled down the tattered NASCAR memorabilia her father had tacked to the far wall, but she'd been met with such protest that she'd had to put it all back up.

She set the box down and picked up the chalkboard on the diner counter. She wrote the names of the day's cakes on the board: traditional Southern red velvet cake and peach pound cake, but also green tea and honey macaroons and cranberry doughnuts. She knew the more unusual things would sell out first. It had taken nearly a year, but she'd won over her regulars with her skill with what they already knew, so now they would try anything she made.

Sawyer walked out just as she set the chalkboard back on the counter. "I told Stella I'd come over with pizza tonight. You'll be there?"

"I'm always there. Why don't the two of you sleep together and get it over with?" Sawyer's Thursday pizza courtship of Stella had been going on ever since Julia had moved back to Mullaby. Stella swore there was nothing going on, but Julia thought Stella was being naïve.

Sawyer leaned in close. "Stella and I did sleep together," he said into her ear. "Three years ago, right after her divorce. And before you think that sounds indiscriminate, I try to keep my actions regret-free these days."

She gave him a sharp look as he walked away. His casual, almost flippant, mention of it took her by surprise and made her feel cool and tart, like tasting lime for the first time.

She couldn't blame him for being a scared teenager when he'd found out she'd gotten pregnant from their one night together on the football field all those years ago. She'd been a scared teenager, too. And they'd made the only decisions they were capable of making at the time. For better or worse.

But she resented how easily he'd gotten on with his life. It had been just one night to him. One regretful night with the freaky, unpopular girl he'd barely even talked to at school. A girl who'd been madly in love with him.

Oh, God. She wasn't going to fall into this role again. She couldn't.

Six months and counting and she would leave this crazy place and never think of Sawyer again.

With any luck.

Chapter 2

*W*hen Emily woke, her hairline was wet with sweat and she felt bone tired. She also had absolutely no idea where she was. She sat up quickly and pulled the earbuds of her MP3 player out of her ears. She looked around the room—the lilac wallpaper, the tattered princess furniture. That's when she remembered. She was in her mother's old bedroom.

She'd never slept in a place that felt so hollow. Even though she knew her grandfather was downstairs, having the entire upstairs to herself made her uneasy. All night, there had been long periods of quiet punctuated by loud wooden pops of the house settling. And leaves kept rattling outside her balcony door. She'd finally turned on her MP3 player and tried to imagine herself someplace else. Someplace not so *humid*.

Scared or not, tonight she was going to have to sleep with the balcony doors open, or else perish into a puddle of perspiration. At some point last night, she'd kicked the bedsheet aside. And she'd started out in pajamas, but she'd wiggled out of the bottom part soon after turning in, and was now in only the top. Her mother might have been the most politically correct person on the planet—an activist, an environmentalist, a crusader for the underdog—but even *she* ran the air conditioner when it got too hot.

26

She made her way to the antiquated bathroom and took a bath because there was no shower. And she was momentarily stumped by the fact that there were separate faucets for hot and cold water instead of both coming out of the same faucet like in a normal bathroom.

Afterward she dressed in shorts and a racer-back tank, then went downstairs.

She noticed the note taped to the inside of the screen door right away.

Emily: This is Grandpa Vance writing you. I forgot to tell you that I go out for breakfast every morning. Didn't want to wake you. I'll bring you something back, but there's also teenager food in the kitchen.

The note was written in large block letters that slanted off the lines of the paper, as if he couldn't see around his hand as he was writing.

She took a deep breath, still trying to rearrange her expectations. Her first day here, and he didn't want to spend it with her.

Standing at the screen door, Emily heard a swish of leaves and, startled, looked up to see a woman in her thirties walking up the front porch steps. She had light brown hair that was cut into a beautiful swinging bob just below her ears. Emily could never get her own bobbed hair to look like that. She'd been trying to grow it out forever, and could only manage a short ponytail with it. And even then, it fell out of the tail and around her face most of the time.

The woman didn't see Emily standing there until she reached the top step. She instantly smiled. "Hello! You must be Vance's granddaughter," she said as she came to a stop at the door. She had pretty, dark brown eyes.

"Yes, I'm Emily Benedict."

"I'm Julia Winterson. I live over there." She turned her head slightly, indicating the yellow and white house next door. That's when Emily noticed the pink streak in Julia's hair, tucked behind her ear. It wasn't something she expected from someone so fresh-faced, in flour-stained jeans and a white peasant blouse. "I brought you an apple stack cake." She opened the white box she was holding and showed Emily what looked like a stack of very large brown pancakes with some sort of filling in between each one. "It means . . ." she struggled with the word, then finally said, "welcome. I know Mullaby has its faults, as I'm sure your mother told you, but it's also a town of great food. You're going to eat very well while you're here. At least there's that."

Emily couldn't remember the last time she'd had an appetite for anything, much less food, but she didn't tell Julia that. "My mother didn't tell me anything about Mullaby," Emily said, staring at the cake.

"Nothing?"

"No."

Julia seemed shocked into silence.

"What?" Emily looked up from the cake.

"It's nothing," Julia said, shaking her head. She closed the lid on the box. "Do you want me to put this in the kitchen?"

"Sure. Come in," Emily said as she opened the screen door for her.

As Julia walked in, she noticed the note from Grandpa Vance still on the screen. "Vance asked me to take him grocery shopping yesterday morning so he could get some things for you," she said, nodding toward the note. "His idea of teenager food was Kool-Aid, fruit roll-ups, and gum. I convinced him to buy chips, bagels, and cereal, too."

"That was nice of you," Emily said. "To take him shopping, I mean."

"I was a big fan of the Giant of Mullaby when I was a kid." When Emily looked at her, not understanding, Julia explained, "That's what people around here call your grandfather."

"How tall *is* he?" Emily asked, her voice hushed, as if he might hear.

Julia laughed. It was a great laugh, and hearing it was like stepping into a spot of sunshine. That she came bearing cake seemed oddly fitting. It was like she was *made* of cake, light and pretty and decorated on the outside—with her sweet laugh and pink streak to her hair—but it was anyone's guess what was on the inside. Emily suspected it might be something dark. "Tall enough to see into tomorrow. That's what he tells everyone. He's over eight feet tall. I know that much. World record keepers came nosing around here once, but Vance wouldn't have anything to do with them."

Julia knew the way to the kitchen, so Emily followed. The kitchen was large and kitschy, like something straight out of the 1950s. Years ago, it must have been a showplace. It was overwhelmingly red—red countertops, red and white tile floor, and a large red refrigerator that had a sliver pull handle, like a meat locker. Julia put the cake box on the counter, then turned to stare at Emily for a moment. "You look a lot like your mother," she finally said.

"You knew her?" Emily asked, perking up at the thought of finding someone willing to talk about her mother.

"We were in the same class in school. But we weren't close." Julia stuffed her hands into her jeans pockets. "She didn't tell you *anything*?"

"I knew she was born in North Carolina, but I didn't know where. I didn't even know I had a grandfather." Julia's eyebrows rose and Emily found herself rushing to explain. "She never *said* I didn't have one, she just never talked about him and I always assumed it was because he had passed away. Mom didn't like to talk about her past, and I respected that. She always said there was no use dwelling on the unfixable past when there was so much you could do to fix the future. She devoted all her time to her causes."

"Her causes?"

"Amnesty International. Oxfam. Greenpeace. The Nature Conservancy. She traveled a lot when she was younger. After I was born, she settled down in Boston. She was very involved locally there."

"Well. That's . . . not what I expected."

"Was she like that here? Was she involved in a lot of causes?"

Julia quickly took her hands out of her pockets. "I should be going."

"Oh," Emily said, confused. "Well, thank you for the cake."

"No problem. My restaurant is called J's Barbecue, on Main Street. Come by anytime for the best cake in Mullaby. The barbecue is really good, too, but I can't take credit for it. That's where your grandfather is right now, by the way. He walks there every morning for breakfast."

Emily followed Julia to the front door. "Where is Main Street?"

As they stepped onto the porch, Julia pointed. "At the end of Shelby Road here, turn left onto Dogwood. About a half-mile later, turn right. You can't miss it." Julia started toward the steps, but Emily stopped her.

31

"Wait, Julia. I saw some sort of light in the back-yard last night. Did you see it?"

Julia turned. "You've seen the Mullaby lights already?"

"What are the Mullaby lights?"

Julia scratched her head and tucked her hair behind her ears, as if deciding what to say. "They're white lights that sometimes dart through the woods and fields around here. Some say it's a ghost that haunts the town. It's just another town oddity," she said, as if there were many. "Don't pay any attention to it and it will go away."

Emily nodded.

Julia turned to leave again, but stopped with her back to Emily. She finally turned back around and said, "Listen, I'll be next door if you ever need me, at least for the next six months. This place takes some getting used to. Believe me, I know."

Emily smiled and she felt her shoulders lose some tension. "Thanks."

IT DIDN'T take Emily long to decide to walk to Main Street and greet her grandfather. She thought it would be nice to walk home with him, establish some sort of routine. He'd obviously lived alone for a long time, so maybe his hesitancy around her came from simply not knowing how to act. *Don't wait for the world to change, Emily,* her mother used to say to her, sometimes in a frustrated voice. *Change it yourself!*

Emily wondered if her mother had been disappointed in her. She didn't have her mother's passion, her courage, her drive. Emily was cautious, but her mother had never met a person she didn't want to help. It had been an awkward dynamic. Emily had always been in awe of her mother, but it had been hard to get close to her. Dulcie had wanted to help, but never be helped.

She found Main Street easily. Just like Julia said, there really was no missing it. Once she turned the corner off Dogwood, there was an enormous sign declaring that she was now on "Historic Main Street." It was a long, beautiful street, different from the comfortable neighborhoods she'd walked through to get there. The street began with brick mansions in grand Federal style, sitting close to the sidewalk with almost no front yards to speak of. Across the street from the mansions was a park with a bandstand that had a lovely silver crescent-moon weathervane on top of it. Past the houses and the park, the street turned commercial, with a series of touristy shops and restaurants squeezed side by side into old brick buildings. Emily counted seven barbecue restaurants, and she was only halfway down the business end of street. *Seven.* They were obviously the source of the smell that settled over the town like a veil. Woody, sweet smoke was rising from behind some of the restaurants in wisps and curls.

There were a lot tourists around, mesmerized, as

she was, by Mullaby's old-fashioned beauty. The sidewalks were crowded, more crowded than she'd expected at that time of morning. She kept looking, but she couldn't see J's Barbecue and, out of nowhere, panic set in. One moment she was feeling happy and proactive, walking along this beautiful street, and the next moment she was terrified that she couldn't find the restaurant she was looking for. What if Julia had been wrong? What if Grandpa Vance wasn't here? What if she couldn't find her way back?

She started to feel light-headed. It was like being underwater, this pressure against her eyes and ears, always followed by sparkling confetti swimming along her periphery.

She'd been having these anxiety attacks ever since her mother died. It was easy enough to hide them from Merry, her mother's best friend, with whom Emily had lived for the past four months. All she had to do was close her bedroom door. And at school, her teachers would turn a blind eye when she stayed in the girls' restroom, sitting on the floor by the sinks trying to catch her breath, instead of coming to class.

The business end of Main Street was lined with benches, so she made it to the nearest one and sat. She'd broken out into a cold sweat. She wouldn't faint. She *wouldn't*.

She leaned forward and rested her chest against her thighs, her head down. *The length of the thigh-*

bone is indicative of overall height. It was a random thought, something she remembered from physiology class.

A pair of expensive men's loafers suddenly appeared on the sidewalk in front of her.

She slowly looked up. It was a young man about her age, wearing a white summer linen suit, the jacket pushed away from his hips by his hands resting casually in his trouser pockets. He had on a red bow tie and his dark hair was curling around his starched collar. He was handsome in a well-bred kind of way, like something out of a Tennessee Williams play. She unexpectedly felt self-conscious in her shorts and racer-back tank top. Compared to him, she looked like she'd just come from a spin class.

He didn't say anything to her at first, just stared at her. Then he finally, almost reluctantly, asked, "Are you all right?"

She didn't understand. Everyone she'd met here so far treated her as if associating with her was going to hurt. She took a deep breath, the oxygen going to her head with the force of floodwater. "Fine, thanks," she said.

"Are you sick?"

"Just light-headed." She looked down at her feet, in ankle socks and cross-trainers, and seemed strangely detached from herself. *Socks that only cover the ankle are not acceptable. Socks must be crew or knee socks only.* So said the Roxley School for Girls handbook. She'd been at Roxley School all her school career. Her mother had helped found it, a school to empower girls, encouraging activism and volunteerism.

Silence. She looked up again and the young man was gone, like smoke. Had she been hallucinating? Maybe she'd conjured up some out-of-time Southern archetype to go along with her surroundings. After a few minutes, she put her elbows on her knees and lifted herself just slightly.

She felt someone take a seat beside her on the bench and she caught a nice, clean scent of cologne. The loud aluminum crack of a soda can being opened startled her, and she sat all the way up with a jerk.

The young man in the white linen suit had returned. He was sitting beside her now, extending a can of Coke.

"Go on," he said. "Take it."

She reached for the can, her hand shaking slightly. She took a long drink and it was cold, sweet, and so sharp it made her tongue burn. She couldn't remember the last time something had tasted this good. She couldn't stop drinking. In no time she had emptied the can.

When she finished, breathless, she closed her eyes and pressed the cold can against her forehead. When was the last time she'd had something to drink? When she thought back, it was long before she'd gotten on the bus in Boston yesterday.

She heard a crackling of paper. The young man said, "Don't be alarmed," and she felt something cold on the back of her neck. Freezing. Her hand went instantly to her neck, covering his hand with hers.

"What is that?" she demanded.

"I believe it's a Creamsicle," he said, leaning back to look at it. "It was the first thing I grabbed from the freezer in the general store."

For the first time, she noticed that they were sitting in front of a deliberately old-fashioned place called Zim's General Store. The door was propped open and Emily could see large barrels of candy near the cash register, and an entire wall of vintage reproduction tin signs in the back.

"It's mostly for the tourists, so it's been a long time since I've been in there," he said. "But it still smells like cinnamon and floor polish. Are you still with me? How are you feeling?"

She turned back to him and realized just how close he was, close enough to see that his ivy-green irises were rimmed in black. Strangely, she thought she could actually *feel* him, feel a sort of energy emanating from him, like heat from a fire. He was so odd and lovely. For a moment, she was completely under his spell. She'd been staring at him for a while before she realized what she was doing. Then she also realized her hand was still on his on her neck. She slowly moved her hand and shifted away. "I'm fine now. Thank you."

He took the paper-covered Creamsicle off her neck and held it out to her, but she shook her head. He shrugged and unwrapped it. He took a bite as he sat back and crossed his legs, studying the store in front of them. She almost wished she'd taken the Creamsicle now. It looked delicious—cool vanilla and sharp bright orange.

"I'm Emily Benedict," she said, extending her hand.

He didn't turn to her, nor did he take her hand. "I know who you are." He took another bite of the Creamsicle.

Emily's hand fell to her lap. "You do?"

"I'm Win Coffey. My uncle was Logan Coffey."

She looked at him blankly. This was obviously something he thought she should know. "I just moved here."

"Your mother didn't tell you?"

Her mother? What did her mother have to do with this? "Tell me what?"

He finally turned to her. "Good God. You really don't know."

"Know what?" This was beginning to concern her.

He stared at her for an uncomfortably long time. "Nothing," he finally said as he threw away what was left of the Creamsicle in a receptacle by the bench, then stood. "If you're not feeling well enough to walk home on your own, I can call our driver to take you."

"I'll be fine." She lifted the can slightly. "Thank you for the Coke."

He hesitated. "I'm sorry I refused to shake your hand. Forgive me." He held out his hand. Confused, she took it. She was immediately shocked by the warmth of him, stretching out to her like wandering vines. He made her feel *tangled* in him, somehow. It wasn't exactly a bad feeling, just strange.

He released her hand and she watched him walk down the sidewalk. His skin almost glowed in the morning summer sun, which was slanting across the buildings in blinding golds and tangerines. He looked so alive, shining with it.

For a moment, she couldn't look away.

"Emily?"

She turned and saw her giant grandfather walking toward her carrying a paper bag. People were parting on the sidewalk, watching him in awe. She could tell he was trying not to notice, but his enormous shoulders were hunched, as if attempting to make himself smaller.

She stood and tossed the can of Coke into a nearby recycling container. Vance came to a stop in front of her. "What are you doing here?" he asked.

"I thought I'd meet you so we could walk home together."

The look on his face was almost indecipherable, but if she had to guess, she'd just made him *sad*. She was horrified.

"I'm sorry," she immediately said. "I didn't mean to—"

"Was that Win Coffey you were talking to?"

"Do you know him?"

Vance stared down the sidewalk. Emily couldn't see Win anymore, but Vance's height obviously gave him an advantage. "Yes, I know him," he said. "Let's go home."

"I'm sorry, Grandpa Vance."

"Don't apologize, child. You did nothing wrong. Here, I brought you an egg sandwich from the restaurant." He handed the bag to her.

"Thank you."

He nodded and put one impossibly long arm around her, then walked her home in silence.

Chapter 3

You'll never guess who I met today," Win Coffey said as he stood in front of the large sitting room window and watched a whale of gray sky swallow the pink evening light.

There was a sound of ticking heels on the white marble floor of the foyer, and Win could see the reflection of his mother as she entered the room, followed by Win's younger sister. His mother sat beside his father on the couch, and his sister crossed the room to the settee.

Win's father, Morgan, folded his newspaper and set it aside. He took off his reading glasses and focused on Win, not his wife. It had been a long time since Win's parents had really looked at each other. They seemed like ghosts to each other now, only ever seen out of the corners of their eyes. "Who did you meet?"

Right on schedule, the blinds began to automatically lower in the sitting room. Win waited until the window was completely covered, shutting out his view, before turning around. The room smelled of cold oranges and was filled with antique furniture—Federal-style highboys and couches tastefully upholstered in blue and gray florals. It was just so old, so familiar. Nothing ever changed. "Emily Benedict."

Her name was instantly recognized. His father's anger was sudden and tangible. It charged the air with hot currents.

Win silently returned his father's stare, not backing down. It was something Morgan himself had taught him. And they had been butting heads enough lately that this was a familiar dance.

"Win, you know my brother would be alive today if it weren't for her mother," Morgan said tightly. "And our secret would still be safe."

"No one in town has ever said a word about that night," Win said calmly.

"But they know. That puts us at their mercy." Morgan used his reading glasses to point at Win. "And no one should be more angry than you, the first generation to grow up with everyone knowing, with everyone looking at you differently."

Win sighed. It was something his father could never understand. Win *wasn't* angry. If anything, he was frustrated. If everyone knew, why did no one talk about it? Why did his family still stay in at night? Why did they cling to traditions that simply didn't make sense anymore? If people looked at Win differently, it was because of that, not because of the story of some strange affliction the Coffeys had, seen only once, over twenty years ago. Who was to say things couldn't be different now? No one had even tried.

"I don't think Emily knows," Win said. "I don't think her mother told her."

"Stop," his father warned. "Whatever you're thinking. Stop. Emily Benedict is off-limits. End of discussion."

A woman in a white dress and apron entered the room, carrying a tray with a silver tea service. Win's father gave him a look that meant *Be quiet now*. They rarely talked about it among themselves—in fact Win sometimes thought his mother had even forgotten and she seemed strangely happier that way—but they never, *ever* talked about it in front of the help.

Win turned and walked over to where his sister, Kylie, was sitting in the far corner of the room. She had her phone out and was texting someone. This was traditionally reading time in the Coffey household, at dusk, just before dinner. It was an old family tradition, dating back hundreds of years, structuring their time at night when they were all forced to stay inside because of their secret, even on beautiful summer nights like this one. Win didn't see the point of it now, and he was itching to go outside. He'd felt this building for months now. He didn't want to sneak around like there was something wrong with him anymore.

He sat beside his sister and watched her ignore him for a few minutes. Win was almost two years older than Kylie, and when they were kids, she used to follow him around relentlessly. She was about to turn sixteen and she still followed him, either to vex him or to protect him. He wasn't sure which. He wasn't sure she knew, either. "You shouldn't test him," Kylie said. "If I were you, I'd stay far, far away from that girl."

"Maybe I'm just getting to know my enemy." It was unsettling, his unexpected fascination with Emily, with her unruly blond hair and the sharp edges of her face and body. When they'd shaken hands that morning, he hadn't wanted to let go. There was something vulnerable about her, something soft under those sharp edges. He'd been thinking about her all day. It had to be more than a coincidence, Dulcie Shelby's daughter coming to town at the same time he was having issues with the way his family chose to live. Maybe it was a sign.

Yes. That was it.

It had to be a sign.

"I'm going out again tonight," he said suddenly. "Don't tell Dad. And don't follow me."

Kylie rolled her eyes. "Why do you keep trying? I can tell you from experience, it's not all that great."

"What?"

"Being ordinary."

"JULIA! WILL you get the door please?" Stella called from downstairs that same evening, just as Julia was taking her second attempt at madeleines out of the oven. She frowned at the pan. Still no good.

Stella bellowed again, "Julia! It's Sawyer, and I'm in the bathtub!"

Julia sighed. She'd already seen Sawyer once today. That was enough. The key to getting out of this stay in Mullaby unscathed was not associating with him.

Julia wiped her hands on her jeans and went downstairs with hard, Godzilla footfalls on the steps to annoy Stella, whose bathroom was directly under the staircase. Through the sheer curtains on the front door window, she could see a figure haloed by the porch light.

She took a deep breath and opened the door. But she smiled in relief when she saw who it was.

Emily shifted from one foot to the other. She was wearing the same clothes she'd been wearing that

44

morning, black shorts and a black tank top, and her quirky blond hair shone like meringue in the light by the door. "Hi, Julia," she said. "Am I interrupting something?"

"No. No, of course not." She stepped back and waved Emily in. When Julia had told her that she'd be here if Emily ever needed her, she didn't think she'd take her up on her offer so soon. Still, as Julia watched the girl look around awkwardly, her heart went out to her. It was never easy being the outsider, especially when it wasn't by choice.

"You have a nice house," Emily said. Stella's part of the house was warm and lovely, thanks to her decorator mother—golden wood floors, lively flower arrangements, original artwork, and a striped silk couch she wouldn't let anyone sit on.

"It's not mine. It belongs to my friend Stella. I have the apartment upstairs."

As if on cue, Stella yelled, "Hello, Sawyer! I'm wearing nothing but steam, want to see?"

"It's not Sawyer," Julia called to her. "I can't believe you're waiting for him in the bathtub. Get out before you turn into a prune." Emily's brows rose and Julia said, "That's Stella. Don't ask. Come on, I'll show you my part of the house." She started up the stairs and motioned Emily to follow.

At the top of the staircase, Julia had to step back in the narrow hallway to let Emily enter, then she reached around her to close the door.

"Just let me turn off the stove," she said as she

walked to the bedroom that had been turned into a tiny kitchen. There was a mood of magic and frenzy to the room. Crystalline swirls of sugar and flour still lingered in the air like kite tails. And then there was the smell—the smell of hope, the kind of smell that brought people home. Tonight it was the comfort of browning butter and the excitement of lemon zest.

The window in the room was wide open, because that was the way Julia always baked. Bottling up the smell made no sense. The message needed some way out.

"What are you making?" Emily asked from the doorway as Julia turned off the stove.

"I experiment with recipes here before I make them for the restaurant. My madeleines aren't up to snuff yet." Julia picked up a madeleine from her first batch. "See? Madeleines should have a distinct hump on this side. This is too flat. I don't think I refrigerated my batter long enough." She took Emily's hand and placed the small spongy cake in her palm. "This is how the French serve madeleines, with the shell side down, like a boat. In America, we like to see the pretty shell side from the shape of the madeleine pan, so we serve them this way." She turned the madeleine over. "Go on, try it."

Emily took a bite and smiled. She covered her lips with her hand and said, her mouth full, "You're a really good cook."

"I've had a lot of practice. I've been baking since I was sixteen."

"It must be nice to have such a gift."

Julia shrugged. "I can't take credit for it. Someone else gave it to me." Sometimes she resented the fact that she never would have found this skill on her own, that she had only discovered what she was truly good at because of someone else. She had to keep reminding herself that it didn't matter how the skill got there, it was what she did with it, the love that came out of it, that mattered. Emily looked like she was going to ask what Julia meant, so Julia quickly said, "How was your first full day here?"

One more bite and Emily had finished the madeleine. She took a moment to chew and swallow, then said, "I guess I'm confused."

Julia crossed her arms over her chest and leaned a hip against the ancient, olive-drab refrigerator. "About what?"

"About why my mom left. About why she didn't stay in touch with people here. Did she have friends? What was she like when she lived here?"

. Julia paused with surprise. Emily had a lot to learn about this town, about the havoc her mother had wreaked. But Julia certainly wasn't going to be the one who told her. "Like I said, I didn't know her well," Julia said carefully. "We weren't in the same social group in school, and I had my own problems at the time. Have you talked to your grandfather? He's the one you should ask."

"No." Emily tucked back some of her short, fly-away hair. Her whole demeanor was so achingly sincere. "He's been hiding in his room all day. Did he and my mom not get along? Do you think that's why she never came back?"

"No, I don't think that's it. Everyone gets along with Vance. Come sit down." Julia put her arm around Emily's shoulder and led her out of the kitchen bedroom and into the living room bedroom. This room contained the only nice thing in her apartment—a royal blue love seat Stella's mother had given her from her decorator's showroom. There was also a television on an old coffee table and a rickety bookcase full of pots and pans—overflow from the kitchen. Julia had put most of her stuff in Baltimore in storage when she'd moved here, and brought only her clothes and her cooking supplies, so there wasn't much to the apartment. It was shabby and sparse, which was fine with her. There was no sense in getting comfortable. When they sat down, Julia said, "All I can tell you is that your mother was the most beautiful, popular girl in school. She made it seem effortless. Perfect clothes. Perfect hair. Supremely confident. She was in a group that called themselves Sassafras, made up of girls in school whose families had money. I wasn't one of them."

Emily looked astonished. "My mom was popular? Grandpa Vance had money?"

There was a knock at her door. "Excuse me," Julia said as she got up. She assumed it was Stella, which was why her whole body gave a start when she opened the door, felt a gust of air that smelled like freshly cut grass, and saw Sawyer standing at the top of the staircase.

"I brought pizza," he said with a smile. "Come down."

Something was definitely afoot. A year and a half of Thursday night get-togethers, and Sawyer had never asked her to come down to have pizza with him and Stella before. "Thanks, but I can't." She took a step back to close the door.

He tilted his head at her. "If I didn't know better, I'd think you were embarrassed."

That got her. "Embarrassed? By what?"

"By the fact that I now know you've been baking cakes for me."

She snorted. "I never said I baked them *for* you. I said I baked them *because* of you."

"So you *did* say it," he said.

She met his eyes. Yes, she'd said it. And as much as she wished it weren't true, it was. The one night they'd had together, they'd lain side by side on the high school football field, staring up at a starry night she'd never seen the likes of before or since, and he'd told her a story of how his mother used to bake cakes on summer afternoons and, no matter where he'd been, it had sent him to her, a beacon of powdered sugar flowing

49

like pollen in the wind. He'd sensed it, he'd said. He'd *seen* it.

Cakes had the power to call. She'd learned that from him.

"Actually, what I think I said was I baked cakes because of *people like* you," she finally said. "You're my target customer, after all."

He looked like he didn't believe her. But he smiled anyway. "That's a nice save."

"Thank you."

His eyes went over her shoulder. He'd never been in her apartment before, and she wasn't going to ask him in now. Sawyer had grown up with money, and she hadn't. But her things in Baltimore were nice—a little edgy, a little bohemian. That's who she was now. Not this. She didn't want him to see this. "It smells good up here," he said. "I want to live in your kitchen."

"There's not enough room. And I only bake here on Thursdays."

"I know. Stella told me when you first moved in. Why do you think I always come by on Thursdays?"

She'd never even suspected. He was that good. "I can't come down, because I have company. You and Stella have fun." She closed the door and leaned against it, letting out a deep breath. After a moment, she realized that she hadn't heard Sawyer walk back down. She turned her head and put her ear to the door. Was he still there? Finally there was a whisper of movement and she heard him walk away.

She pushed herself from the door and went back to the living room. "Sorry about that."

"I can come back later if you're busy," Emily said.

"Don't be silly."

"So, everyone must have liked my mom, if she was so popular."

Julia hesitated. But before she could speak, there was another knock at the door. "Excuse me again."

"Who do you have up here?" Stella demanded when Julia opened the door. Stella had a wide, exotic face, with almond-shaped eyes and straight dark brows. She was wearing a kimono-style robe and her dark hair was pulled up into a bun. Some tendrils, still wet from her bath, were sticking to her neck. "Sawyer said you had company. Are you seeing someone? Why didn't you tell me? Who is it?"

"It's none of your business," she said because she knew it would drive Stella crazy. She still hadn't forgiven her for telling Sawyer about the cakes. And Julia thought it was rich for Stella to demand to know if Julia was seeing someone, when Stella had *slept with Sawyer* three years ago and had never told her.

She closed the door, but as soon as she walked back into the living room, the knocking started again. Incessantly. Stella had a wild hair now.

"She's not going to stop until she meets you," Julia said to Emily. "Do you mind?"

Emily seemed game, and followed her into the hallway.

As soon as Julia opened the door again, Stella said, "I'm not leaving until . . ." She stopped when Julia opened the door farther, revealing Emily standing beside her.

"This is Vance Shelby's granddaughter," Julia said. "Emily, this is Stella Ferris."

Stella seemed incapable of speech.

"Emily came by wanting to know what her mother was like when she lived here."

Stella recovered quickly. "Well, it's so lovely to meet you, Emily! Sawyer and I were friends with your mother. Come downstairs and have pizza with us. I'll pull out my yearbooks."

When Stella stepped to the side, Emily didn't hesitate and bounded down the stairs. With the elegant lines of her face and her tall, willowy body, it was easy to forget how young she was, until she did something like that.

Before Stella could follow, Julia grabbed the sleeve of her robe. "Don't talk about what her mother did."

Stella looked insulted. "What's the matter with you? I'm not an ogre."

Emily waited eagerly for them to come down. Once they did, Stella led the way to her kitchen, her robe billowing dramatically behind her.

Sawyer had his back to them and was staring out the kitchen window, his hands in his pockets. He turned when he heard them enter. His brows shot up when he saw Emily.

"Hello, who is this very lovely young lady?" He pronounced the word "very" *Vera,* like it was a proper noun, the name of a pretty woman who wore white gloves. There was something inherent in Stella's and Sawyer's manners around strangers, something that always gave away their breeding.

"This is who Julia was entertaining, Sawyer, so you can stop pouting. This is Emily, *Dulcie Shelby's daughter,*" Stella said significantly.

Sawyer didn't miss a beat. "A pleasure." Sawyer held out his hand and Emily shook it. She actually giggled a little, and Emily didn't strike Julia as a giggler. "Let's eat the pizza while it's hot. Julia?" Sawyer walked over to the kitchen table and pulled out a chair for her, not giving her much of a choice.

Stella set out drinks and paper napkins, then they unceremoniously ate the vegetarian pizza out of the box. Julia tried to eat a slice quickly so she could leave. Sawyer was casual and relaxed, smiling at her like he knew what she was doing. Stella was as comfortable wearing a robe at the dinner table as she would have been in a Dior suit. And Emily was watching the three of them like they were unopened presents.

"So, you two knew my mom?" Emily finally asked, as if she couldn't wait any longer.

53

"We knew her well," Stella said. "Dulcie and I were in a close-knit group of friends."

"Sassafras?" Emily said.

"Right. Sawyer dated a girl named Holly who was in the group, so he was one of our honorary boys."

"You weren't friends with Julia?"

"I wasn't friends with anyone back then," Julia said.

Emily turned to her, curious. She had pizza sauce on her upper lip. Julia smiled and handed her a napkin. "Why not?" Emily said, wiping her mouth.

"Being a teenager is tough. We all know that. Sassafras made it look easy. I looked like the truth."

"What did Sassafras do?" Emily asked. "Community service? Fundraising?"

Stella laughed. "We weren't that kind of group. Let me get the yearbooks." She tossed her pizza crust into the box, then left the kitchen. She swished back in minutes, possibly the only person in the world who knew where to find her high school yearbooks without digging through closets or calling her parents. "Here we are." She set a green and silver book emblazoned with the words HOME OF THE FIGHTING CATS! on the table in front of Emily, then opened it. "That's Sassafras, with your mother in the middle, of course. We held court on the front steps of the school every morning before classes. There's your mother at homecoming. There she is as our prom queen. There's Sawyer on the soccer team."

Sawyer shook his head. "I rarely played."

Stella cut her eyes at him. "That's because you didn't want to risk hurting that face."

"A valid excuse."

Stella turned the next page. "And there's Julia."

It was a photo of her eating lunch by herself on the top row of the bleachers on the football field. That was Julia's domain. Before school, at lunch, when she skipped classes, sometimes even at night, that was her safe place.

"Look how long your hair was! And it was all pink!" Emily said, then looked closer. "Are you wearing black lipstick?"

"Yes."

"No one knew what to think of Julia back then," Stella said.

Julia smiled and shook her head. "I was harmless."

"To other people, maybe," Sawyer murmured, and Julia automatically pulled her long sleeves farther down her arms.

"Julia's father sent her to boarding school after our sophomore year," Stella told Emily, and Julia turned back to them. "She didn't come back for a long time. And when she did, no one recognized her."

"I did," Sawyer said.

Stella rolled her eyes. "Of course *you* did."

Emily was poring over the yearbook now, flipping through pages, stopping every time she came across a photo of her mother. "Look!" she said. "Mom is wearing her charm bracelet! This one!" Emily held up her wrist.

Julia found herself staring at Emily's profile, a familiar yearning in her heart. Without thinking, she reached over and pushed some of Emily's hair out of her eyes. Emily didn't seem to notice, but when Julia looked across the table, Sawyer and Stella were staring at her like she'd just grown another head.

"Who is this with my mom?" Emily asked, pointing to an elegant dark-haired boy in a suit and bow tie. "He's in a lot of pictures with her."

"That's Logan Coffey," Julia said.

"*That's* who he was talking about." Emily sat back and smiled. "I met a boy named Win Coffey today. He mentioned that his uncle was Logan Coffey. He seemed surprised that I didn't know who he was."

Oh, hell, Julia thought. *That can't be good.*

"Was Logan Coffey her boyfriend?" Emily asked.

"We all wondered. He and Dulcie denied it," Julia said cautiously. "Basically, he was just a shy, mysterious boy your mother tried to coax out of his shell."

"Does he still live here? Do you think I could talk to him about my mom?"

There was a conspicuous silence. No one wanted to tell her. Julia finally said, "Logan Coffey died a long time ago, sweetheart."

"Oh." As if sensing the change in atmosphere, Emily reluctantly closed the book. "I guess I should get back home. Thank you for letting me look through the yearbook."

Stella waved her hand. "Take it with you. That was twenty pounds ago. I don't need to be reminded."

"Really? Thank you!" When Emily stood, so did Julia. Julia walked her to the door and said good night, watching until Emily evaporated into the darkness under the canopy of trees next door.

When Julia walked back in, Stella was standing there, her hands on her hips. "Okay, what's going on?"

"What do you mean?"

"Why are you acting that way around her?"

"I'm not acting any way around her." Julia frowned. "Why are you looking at me like that?"

"I'm just surprised, that's all. I mean, come on. You're the least maternal person on the planet." Stella laughed, but stopped when she saw the look on Julia's face. Julia had gotten used to people saying that to her, but it didn't make it any easier to hear. It was the price you paid when you were thirty-six and had no apparent interest in sharing your life with anyone. "Oh, I didn't mean it in a bad way." And Julia knew Stella didn't. Neither did Julia's friends in Baltimore when they said, *You love your independence too much.* Or *You couldn't be a mom because you'd be cooler than your teenager.* "Let's go out on the back porch and have wine."

"No, thanks."

"Julia . . ."

"I know you have something sweet in here," Sawyer called from the kitchen, followed by the banging of cabinet doors.

Stella rolled her eyes. "That man can find my stash of Hershey's Miniatures no matter where I hide them."

"Let him have them before he tries to raid my kitchen," Julia said as she headed for the staircase. "I have work to do."

EMILY SAT on her balcony when she got home, the yearbook on her lap. Earlier that day, she'd gone through the closet and all the drawers in her bedroom, in search of . . . something. Some clue to her mother's time here. She'd begun to feel strangely suspicious, like there was something she needed to know that no one was telling her. But there was only her mother's name on the dusty trunk at the foot of the bed to give any indication that Dulcie had ever even lived there. There was nothing personal. There were no photos, no old letters, not even a scarf or an earring left behind. That's why Emily had gone over to Julia's. She'd felt awkward about it at first, but now she was glad she'd done it. The yearbook was such a treasure, if a little confusing. One of the tenets of Roxley School for Girls was that there was no caste system, no superlatives, no elections. How could her mother have been *prom queen*?

Emily remembered her mother never let her go to the mall because of the open competition there to have something as good as or better than the next person. She always said that fashion should never be a factor in determining someone's self-worth. So of course Roxley School had uniforms. Yet, here in the yearbook, her mother was in the trendiest clothes of the time, and she had *mall hair*.

Maybe she'd been embarrassed by who she'd been as a youth. Maybe she thought her grassroots reputation might have been hurt by her tiara-laden past.

Still, that seemed like such a peculiar reason never to come back.

Emily looked up from the yearbook when she heard voices gliding through the still night, coming from the back porch next door. A woman's laughter. A tinkling of glasses.

Sitting at the old patio table she'd cleared of leaves, she smiled and leaned back. The stars looked twisted in the limbs of the trees, like Christmas lights. She felt like part of the hollow around her was filling. She'd come here with too many expectations. Things weren't perfect, but they were getting better. She'd even made friends next door.

She took a deep breath of the sweet evening heat, and began to get sleepy.

She only meant to close her eyes for a moment.

But she dozed off almost immediately.

WHEN SHE woke up, it was still dark. She blinked a few times, trying to figure out what time it was and how long she'd been asleep.

She looked down and saw the yearbook had fallen from her lap to the leaves on the balcony floor. Her back stiff, she leaned down to retrieve it. When she sat back up, her skin prickled.

The light was back! The light Julia said people thought was a ghost.

Frozen, she watched it in the woodline beyond the old gazebo in Grandpa Vance's backyard. It didn't disappear like it had last night. It lingered instead, darting from tree to tree, hesitating in between.

Was it . . . was it *watching her*?

She quickly looked next door. There were no lights on. No one to see this but her.

She turned back to the light. What *was* that?

She made herself stand and slowly walk into her room. She set the yearbook on the bed and paused for a moment. She didn't know what came over her, but suddenly she took off in a run, her bare feet slapping against the hardwood floors. She slowed down so that she'd be more quiet as she went down the stairs and past Grandpa Vance's room, but then she took off again. She was briefly foiled by the locked kitchen door, but after fumbling with the lock, she finally opened the door and ran out.

The light was still there! She ran after it, into the wooded area behind the gazebo. The light quickly retreated and she heard footsteps in the leaves.

Footsteps?

Ghosts don't have footsteps.

After about five minutes of chasing it through the gloomy, moonlit woods, her hands up to swat away the low-hanging branches, it began to occur to her that she had no idea where she was going, or where this patch of trees ended. When the light suddenly disappeared, she felt the first twinge of real worry. What was she doing? But a few more steps and she unexpectedly broke through the trees. She stood there for a moment, out of breath and painfully aware that she was barefoot. She lifted her foot and saw a fine trickle of blood. She'd cut her heel.

Out of the quiet came the distinct sound of a door being closed.

She jerked her head up and looked around and realized she was on the residential end of Main Street, standing in the middle of the park facing the old brick mansions. The woods behind Grandpa Vance's house must zigzag through other neighborhoods in a crazy labyrinth, ending here, by the bandstand with the crescent moon weathervane. She looked up and down the street, then she looked back into the woods. Surely she saw the light end here?

She limped back home the long way, taking the sidewalks. Her mind was whirling. She couldn't believe she'd just run through the woods in the middle of the night, chasing a so-called ghost. This was so unlike her.

When she reached Grandpa Vance's house, she remembered the front door was still locked, so she had to go around back. She saw a hint of light as she walked to the corner.

The back porch light was now on.

Obviously, Grandpa Vance had heard her run out and was waiting for her. She sighed. It took running around at night to get him to come out of his room. How was she going to explain this? She hobbled up to the kitchen porch and almost tripped over something as she approached the door.

She bent and picked up a box of Band-Aids.

A crunching of leaves invaded the quiet, and she turned with a gasp to see the white light disappearing back into the woods, as if it had never left.

And she would also soon discover that Grandpa Vance had slept through everything.

Chapter 4

*F*rom his bedroom window the next morning, Win watched Vance Shelby walk down the sidewalk toward the business end of Main Street. He was an interesting specimen, if you looked at him scientifically. Win didn't often look at things scientifically. Proof was something he'd learned not to expect from anyone, nor anyone from him. But Vance Shelby looked like a praying mantis, as if biologically suited to grab things, to hide things, to shield. He wouldn't like Win's interest in Emily. It was unfortunate, but it couldn't be avoided.

"Win!" his father called from downstairs. "It's light. Let's go."

Win left his room and walked down the long marble staircase to where his father was waiting in the foyer. Although frequently bored, he didn't mind these outings with his father so much anymore, not like he did when he was a boy. Morgan Coffey liked to get out bright and early to greet shop owners and tourists. From the time Win was about five, Morgan took him with him on these PR treks, to groom him, Win guessed. To let Win know what was expected of him. They went to a different restaurant every morning, where Morgan chatted up everyone. Win just liked the opportunity to get out of the house as soon as possible, at first light. If it had to be with his father, then that was a small price to pay.

"Ready?" Morgan asked when Win met him by the front door.

"If I said no?" Win said as his father opened the door.

Morgan inspected Win, from his red bow tie to his loafers. "You look ready."

"Then I suppose I am."

Morgan took a deep breath, reining in his anger. "Don't get smart with me," he said.

And Win had to concede that it really was too early in the morning for such antagonism.

They walked down the sidewalk. Vance had disappeared—no easy feat for a giant. This morning, Morgan had decided to go to Welchel's Diner. When they entered, he scanned the room quickly, then led Win to a table by the door. Morgan liked to greet people as they came in. He liked to zero in on the tourists, on the people he didn't recognize, first. Win often watched him in awe. For someone so seemingly content with his cloistered life, Morgan Coffey was genuinely thrilled to meet new people. It gave Win hope that, in the end, his father would understand why Win was going to go through with his plans. That's what these mornings were really about, after all. They might be masked in public relations, but it was really all about acceptance.

Win didn't know how long they'd been there—

not long, he supposed, because their breakfast orders hadn't arrived yet—when he saw her.

Emily walked past the diner, staring straight ahead, the sunlight at her back. Her arms and legs were long. She didn't favor her grandfather in any way but this one. But where Vance looked like he'd grown too long, Emily looked . . . perfect.

Win turned to see if his father had noticed. He hadn't. In fact, Morgan had left the table without Win even being aware. He was across the room now, shaking hands with someone. Win turned back to the window, leaning forward to watch Emily walk away. With one last look at his father, he took his napkin out of his lap and set it on the table, then he pushed his chair back and quietly slipped out of the diner.

He followed Emily at a distance, noticing she had on flip-flops that morning, and a Band-Aid on her heel. He stopped when she reached the bench outside of J's Barbecue. She didn't go in, and he wondered why. She didn't look faint, like she'd looked yesterday morning. No, she was waiting. Waiting for her grandfather to come out. The gesture was both charming and uncomfortably lonely.

He was only two or three storefronts away from her, close enough for Emily to look up when Inez and Harriet Jones approached him from behind and said in unison, "Hello, Win!"

He returned Emily's stare before reluctantly turning to Inez and Harriet. They were spinster sisters who lived next door to the Coffey mansion on Main Street. The sisters went everywhere together, wore matching dresses, and carried one purse between them. Long ago, when the Coffeys wanted to put a driveway between the two houses in order to reach the garage behind their house without having to drive around to the next street, the Jones sisters agreed to it on the condition that the Coffeys invite them for drinks every third Tuesday of the month. So, for over thirty years now, the elderly Jones sisters were a fixture on the Coffeys' couch between four and five o'clock, once a month.

"Hello, Miss Jones." He nodded to Inez. "Miss Jones." He nodded to Harriet.

"We saw you staring at that pretty thing there," Inez said, though Win wished she hadn't. Emily could hear every word.

Harriet sucked in her breath suddenly as she clutched her sister's arm. "Sister, do you know who that is?"

"Could it be?" Inez said, clutching her back.

"Yes, it is!" Harriet answered.

"What brings you two out so early this morning?" Win asked, trying to change the subject.

Inez tsked. "Oh, she does look like her mother, doesn't she?"

"She certainly does."

"Can I escort you home?" Win interrupted. "I'm

66

headed that way." He held out his arm, trying to herd them away.

"Her mother had a lot of nerve, sending her here," Inez said. "What a thing to do to a child."

Harriet shook her head. They were both staring at Emily unabashedly. "She's never going to fit in."

"And how is her grandfather going to take care of her? He can barely take care of himself."

"I don't know, Sister," Harriet said. "I don't know."

Win gestured again. "Ladies, shall we?"

Inez wagged her knobby finger at him. "Don't turn into your uncle, Win. Don't get fooled by a pretty face like he did. What a tragedy." The sisters looked at him pityingly. "Stare at her all you want, but stay away. That's what we're going to do. To show support for your family. Right, Sister?"

"It's for the best."

That's when they turned and left him, walking toward home, one arm each looped into the handles of a single handbag, like a yoke between them.

Win closed his eyes for a moment before turning to Emily.

She looked unsettled and he didn't blame her.

He put his hands in his trouser pockets and walked toward her, trying to seem casual and unaffected. "Hello again."

She didn't answer. Her eyes went to the Jones sisters, who were weaving down the sidewalk.

Win hated that they had been so indelicate. "Where is your grandfather? I saw him earlier," he said, to draw her attention away from them.

"Inside," she said. "I'm waiting for him."

"Instead of eating with him?"

"I don't know if he actually wants . . . I just thought I'd wait." She gave him a once-over that tried to be subtle, but wasn't. "Are you always up and dressed like that this early?"

"It's sort of a tradition." He indicated the bench. "May I?"

She nodded. "Where do you come from?" she asked as he sat.

He crossed his legs, trying not to seem too eager, too suspicious. Getting into someone's good graces was second nature to him, but he was nervous. There was so much riding on this. "Here. I'm from here."

She hesitated, as if he'd answered an entirely different question. "No, I meant yesterday and today. Where did you *just* come from?"

He laughed. "Oh. Breakfast with my father. Every morning."

"Does everyone here come to Main Street for breakfast?"

"Not everyone. How is your foot?" he asked, not actually looking at her foot. Instead, he stared into her true blue eyes. She wasn't what he'd expected. Not at all.

"My foot?"

"It looks like you scratched your heel."

She turned her right foot slightly to see the bandaged cut. "Oh. I cut it running barefoot through the woods."

"You should put on shoes next time." She looked back up to see that he was smiling.

She narrowed her eyes. "Thank you. I plan to. Who were those ladies you were talking to?" she asked.

He sighed regretfully. "Inez and Harriet Jones. They're my next-door neighbors."

"Were they talking about me?"

He considered several different answers, but decided to go with "Yes."

"They knew who I was," she said. "They knew my mother."

"Yes."

"Why would they say I wouldn't fit in?"

He shook his head. "If you had cause to worry about them, I would tell you. I promise."

"It sounded like they didn't like my mother."

He picked at imaginary dust on his sleeve. He knew he looked calm, but inside, his heart was knocking against his chest. "If you want me to tell you the story, I will." *God, what was he going to say?* "I think it's better if you know. I'm not sure I should be the one, though. Your mother should have told you. At the very least, your grandfather should have said something by now."

"About what? They mentioned your uncle. Is this about him?"

"Yes. We have history, you and I." He leaned in slightly, conspiratorially. "You just don't know it yet."

She tilted her head curiously. "That's a strange thing to say."

"Just wait. It gets stranger." A flashy older woman in heels and shorts clicked by them. He and Emily both turned to watch her walk to the door of J's Barbecue. That's when Win saw that Vance Shelby was inside, watching them. Not that anyone who knew him could ever be afraid of him, but it was still disconcerting to have someone that large give him such a forceful look. Did Vance know what Win was doing? Emily hadn't noticed, so she seemed surprised when he suddenly stood and said, "I think I should go."

"What? No, wait, tell me about this history. Tell me about my mother and your uncle."

"Next time I see you, I will. Goodbye, Emily," he said as he walked away. It took such restraint to keep from looking back at her until the last possible moment. When he did, right before he entered the diner where he'd left his father, he saw her watching him.

No going back now.

The foundation was set.

She was officially curious.

Chapter 5

*J*ulia had the day's cakes baked and was writing on the chalkboard before there were even four customers in the restaurant. Vance Shelby had arrived and was sitting by himself, waiting for the rest of the old men in his breakfast group. He was drinking his coffee from his saucer instead of his cup, because the lip of the saucer was larger and his giant hand could more easily manage it. Julia was tempted to go talk to him about Emily. But then she thought better of it. It wasn't any of her business. She was only going to be here for a few more months. There was no need to get all knotted up in things. She would be Emily's friend while she was here, and try to help her get settled. That's all she could do.

Vance was watching something outside, a frown on his face.

Julia had just finished writing the names of the day's specials on the board—Milky Way cake, butter pecan cake, cigar-rolled lemon cookies, and vanilla chai macaroons—so she set the chalkboard down and turned to see what had captured Vance's attention.

As soon as she did, the bell over the door rang, and Beverly Dale, Julia's former stepmother, walked in.

At least it wasn't Sawyer.

But it was almost as bad.

"Julia!" Beverly said as she teetered up to the counter in her white kitten heels. "I haven't seen you in a month of Sundays. I always try to get here early enough, but I'm not a morning person, as I'm sure you remember. Last night I said to myself, 'Beverly, you're going to set your alarm and get to the restaurant early enough to see Julia.' And here I am!"

"Congratulations," Julia said, glad that the counter was between them and Beverly couldn't hug her. Beverly could choke an elephant with the scent of her Jean Naté perfume.

"I see you're still wearing those long sleeves," Beverly said, shaking her head. "Bless your heart. I can't imagine you're comfortable, especially in this summertime heat."

"It's cotton. It's not so bad," she said, drawing the sleeves down farther and grasping the cuffs in her hands.

"I understand. Scars aren't pretty on a woman." Beverly leaned in and whispered, "I have a tiny scar here on my forehead that I don't like anyone to see. That's why I have my hairstylist, Yvonne, fix this curl just so."

Julia smiled and nodded, waiting for Beverly to get to what she was really there to talk about.

Julia had been twelve the first time her father had brought Beverly home. He'd told Julia at the time that he thought she needed another female around

72

to talk to about girl things, now that she was growing up—as if he'd brought Beverly into their lives for *her* sake. Beverly had been very attentive to Julia at first. Julia had been a baby when her mother died, so she'd begun to think that maybe having Beverly around *would* be nice. But then Beverly and Julia's father had gotten married, and Julia had actually felt the power shift. Julia's father's attention had been inexorably drawn to the person who'd demanded it the most. And that person had been Beverly. No amount of pouting or temper tantrums, and, later, pink hair or cutting, could ever have competed with Beverly, sexy Beverly with her puff of blond hair, the low V of her shirts, and the high heels she wore even with shorts. She'd liked doing things for Julia's father— cooking his meals, lighting his cigarettes, rubbing his shoulders as he watched television. When Beverly didn't get her way, she'd stop doing those things, and it had been painful for Julia to watch her father try to get back into her good graces.

Beverly and her father had stayed together until about four years ago. When her father had told her about the divorce during Julia's annual Christmas call to him, he'd said in his kind, simple way, "Beverly is such a vibrant woman. She needed more than I could give her."

What she needed, Julia later found out, was a man with cash. Julia's father never had a lot of money, but he'd done very well for a man with only an eighth-grade education. He'd owned his own home and business, free and clear, by the time he was thirty. And he'd been an excellent money manager, which was why Julia had been so shocked when she'd discovered the extent of his debt after his death. She could only assume Beverly had spent her way through what he had, and when there was nothing left, she'd left him for Bud Dale, who had just opened his second muffler shop in town.

Julia remembered seeing Beverly for the first time in years at her father's funeral. She'd aged quite a bit, but she still had that power women with big noses have to seem beautiful, even when they aren't. "I'm sorry about your daddy," she'd said. "Let me know if there's any money left. Some of it should go to me, don't you think? We had twenty beautiful years together." And she'd said it right in front of Bud Dale.

When Julia sold her father's house and took what little was left after paying off the mortgage and applied it to his restaurant mortgage, Beverly had been livid. Some of that money could have gone to her, she'd insisted. But once she realized what Julia was doing, staying here and working to get the restaurant mortgage paid off in order to sell it for a profit, she periodically accosted Julia to remind her that some of the money should go to her, naturally. Like they were in this together.

"Is it always this slow at this hour?" Beverly

asked, waving one of the waitresses over to her. "I'd like two breakfast specials, to go. I'll surprise Bud at work. He'll never believe I'm up this early."

"The place will fill up soon," Julia assured her.

"I hope so. It looks like you're not doing enough to bring in business at breakfast. And you make a lot of desserts." She pointed to the chalkboard. "Do people really eat it all every day? If there's any left over, that's a terrible waste of money."

"There's never any left over. I was just on my way out, Beverly," Julia said. "What can I do for you?"

"Oh, stop with that. You don't have anywhere to go. You never do anything but work and go home. You're so much like your daddy."

Julia tried to hold her smile. At one point in her life, she would have welcomed the comparison. Now, she wanted to scream *No! I've done so much more!*

"I know it's only a few more months until you're going to sell this place. Rumor has it that Charlotte is interested in buying it from you. I just wanted to tell you that I don't think that's a good idea."

"Oh?" Charlotte was the day manager of the restaurant, and the perfect person to sell it to. She not only knew the business, she cared about it. And that meant something to Julia now. When she'd first come back to town, Julia would have gladly sold the restaurant to *anyone* if it had meant a profit. Now that she'd been here awhile, she realized that she owed it to her father to let it go to someone who loved it as much as he had. That's what staying too long had done to her. It had made her soft.

"I think you might give the restaurant to her for less than you should, just because she's worked here a long time. But the whole point is to get as much money as possible for it."

"Thank you for your input, Beverly."

The waitress brought out a bag containing two covered Styrofoam trays. She handed the bag to Beverly, who took it from her without acknowledgment.

"I'll see you soon," Beverly said. "We can go over arrangements. Make it all nice and official, okay?"

Julia didn't say a word, but she had absolutely no intention of giving Beverly any money from the sale of the restaurant. She didn't care how mad Beverly would be when she found out. Julia wouldn't be here to deal with it. It was just easier to let Beverly believe what she wanted to believe. Arguing with her would only make Julia's time here more miserable, and might even hurt business.

Julia and the waitress watched Beverly leave. The waitress—Julia forgot her name—was new. She was holding Beverly's bill in her hand.

"Don't worry about it," Julia said. "She never thinks she has to pay."

The waitress crumpled up the bill, and Julia headed for the door.

Only to have it open, and there was Sawyer.

Julia rubbed her forehead. How could a day be this bad so early?

Sawyer was so bright and attentive, even at this hour. She wondered if he ever slept, or if he simply stayed awake all night, pacing with energy and thinking of new ways to sparkle and charm, new ways to get his way. He met her eyes and smiled. "Julia, you look lovely. Doesn't she look lovely, Granddad?" Sawyer asked the elderly gentleman he was helping through the door.

The old man looked up and smiled. He had deep blue eyes like Sawyer. Alexander men were a sight to behold. "You do look lovely, Julia. That pink streak in your hair adds pizzazz."

Julia smiled at that. "Thank you, Mr. Alexander. Enjoy your breakfast."

"Wait for me, Julia," Sawyer said. "I want to talk to you."

All sorts of warning signals went up, firework flashes in her periphery. "Sorry," she said, and slipped out the door as soon as Sawyer's grandfather had passed by her. "Gotta go."

She walked down the sidewalk toward home. She thought for a moment that she saw Emily down the street, but then she lost sight of her.

Julia knew she could have driven to work, but with most of her money being funneled into the principal payments on the restaurant's mortgage, gas was a luxury. Sometimes her walks home reminded her too much of walking to high school because her father couldn't afford to buy her a car. With envy, she used to watch all the kids who could afford cars drive by. Members of Sassafras, in particular, in their BMWs and Corvettes.

It was all going to be worth it, this sacrifice. She had to keep telling herself that. She had a whole other life waiting for her, one where she could control memories of her past. When she got back to Baltimore, she would pick up where she'd left off and reconnect with friends who only knew her as she was now, not who she'd been then. Nice blank-slate friendships. She'd find a new place to live, get her things out of storage, then find the perfect spot for her bakery. She had worked in other people's bakeries for a long time. When she got her own place, she would bake with all the windows open and make nothing but purple cookies if she wanted to. *Blue-Eyed Girl Bakery.* That was going to be the name. That Julia's eyes were brown didn't matter. It wasn't about her, anyway.

"Julia!" Sawyer called.

She felt a prickle along the back of her neck and picked up her pace. Regardless, Sawyer soon jogged up and fell into step with her.

She cut her eyes at him. "Did you actually run after me?"

He looked indignant, like he'd been caught

doing something uncouth. "I wouldn't have had to if you had waited."

"What do you want?"

"I told you. I want to talk to you."

"So talk," she said.

"Not like this." His hand wrapped around her arm and made her stop. "I've kept my distance since you've been back, because I thought that's what you wanted. When I heard you were moving back to Mullaby, I had . . . hope. But the moment I saw you again, and you gave me a look that could kill, I knew it was still too soon."

"I haven't moved back," she said, wriggling her arm free.

"But I've been doing us both a disservice," he continued, as if she hadn't spoken. "This has gone on too long. I want to talk about it, Julia. I have some things to tell you."

"Talk about what?" she asked.

He was silent.

She tried to laugh it off. "Does this have something to do with thinking I've been baking cakes because of you?"

"I don't know. You tell me."

They stared at each other for a moment before she said, "I have nothing to say to you. And I doubt you have anything to say that I want to hear."

Undeterred, he said, "Have dinner with me on Saturday."

"I have plans on Saturday," she said.

"Oh?" His hands went into his pockets and he rocked back on his heels with surprise. This was a man who wasn't used to being turned down. "With whom?"

"I was thinking of taking Emily to the lake," she said, off the top of her head.

"You're showing a remarkable amount of interest in this girl."

"Does it surprise you that much, Sawyer?" she shot at him. "Really?"

She could tell that hurt him. And it didn't make her feel as good as she thought it would. He hesitated before asking quietly, "Are you ever going to forgive me?"

"I forgave you a long time ago," she said as she turned and walked away. "That doesn't mean I've forgotten."

His voice carried after her. "Neither have I, Julia."

THE WEIGHT of Julia's unhappiness took her breath sometimes when she was sixteen. It had been building for years, brick by brick: adolescence, her father remarrying, her unrequited love for the cutest boy in school, the misfortune of having Dulcie Shelby as a classmate. Still, up until she entered high school, she'd always had friends. She'd always been a good student. She'd always been able to *function*. But then a gradual depression settled over her like someone flipping out a bedsheet and letting it float down to cover her. By the time her sophomore year rolled around, she'd given up on trying to compete with her stepmother, Beverly. Her pink hair and black makeup were attempts to fight the overwhelming sense that she was disappearing. Her friends started avoiding her as her appearance changed and she became more sullen, but she didn't care. She would gladly lose them if it meant her father would just look at her.

It didn't work.

Sometimes she would hear Beverly tell her father not to pay her any attention, that it was just a phase, that she would grow out of it. And of course, he did exactly as Beverly suggested.

Then the cutting started.

Her unhappiness and self-loathing got the better of her one day when she was in her World History class. Mr. Horne was writing something on the whiteboard and Julia was sitting in the back of the room, Dulcie Shelby a few seats in front of her. Julia looked up from doodling in her notebook to see Dulcie whisper something to one of her friends, then take something out of her purse. Seconds later, a small canister of flea powder rolled down the aisle and stopped at Julia's feet.

Dulcie and her friends laughed and Mr. Horne turned around.

He demanded to know what was so funny, but no one in class said a word. Julia kept her eyes down, staring at the canister touching the toe of her Doc Martens knockoffs.

Mr. Horne finally turned back around, and as soon as he did, Julia took the sharpened pencil she was holding and dragged it heavily across her forearm. She didn't realize what she'd done at first. She simply watched the pebbles of blood form on her skin with a weird sense of satisfaction, of release.

At first it was random, using whatever she had on hand, but it soon became more deliberate and she started using razor blades she hid under her mattress at home. Every time she cut herself, it was intense and dramatic, like being jerked from the gaping maw of nothingness and back into life. It not only made her feel, it made her feel *good*. At one point she realized she couldn't stop, that she couldn't get through the day without cutting herself, but she didn't care. She truly didn't care. It wasn't long before her forearms were covered in angry spiderwebs of scabbed-over cuts, and she wore long-sleeved shirts even on the warmest days.

She'd been cutting her arms for months before Julia's father and stepmother found out. It was Beverly who first saw the marks. Julia had just stepped out of the shower one morning and had wrapped a towel around herself, when her stepmother tapped on the door and waltzed in, saying, "Don't mind me. I'm just getting my tweezers—"

She stopped short when she saw Julia's bare arms.

When Julia's father got home from work that evening, he came into her bedroom. His face was pinched and worried and he approached her cautiously, as if trying not to crush her with the weight of his presence. He wanted to know what was wrong, and Julia resented the question. How could he not know?

Her sophomore year ended not long after, and her father and Beverly never let her out of their sight that summer. Instead of feeling like she'd finally gotten what she wanted, she hated that they were trying to stop her from doing the one thing that made her feel better.

The entire summer was one long power struggle. She actually started looking forward to the school year so she could get away from them. And of course, the new school year meant she would get to see Sawyer. Beautiful Sawyer. But just a few days before the start of school at Mullaby High, Julia's father told her that he was sending her away to boarding school. It was a special school, he said. For troubled teens. They were supposed to drive to Baltimore to the school the next day. He'd given her only one day's notice. *One day.* He'd been planning this behind her back all summer!

That night, she crawled out of the laundry room window and ran away. If her father didn't want her around, fine. But she wasn't going to some stupid school. The problem was, she had no idea where else to go. So she ended up on her favorite perch on the high school bleachers.

She'd been there a few hours when Sawyer showed up. It was after midnight, but suddenly there he was, walking around the track. The moon was out and he was wearing white shorts and a white polo, so she could see him clearly from her seat.

She didn't move, so she didn't know what made him look up. But he did, and her breath caught, as it did every time he looked at her in school.

They stared at each other for a long moment. Then he crossed the track and walked up the bleachers toward her.

Sawyer had never approached her before, but he had always watched her at school. A lot of people watched her, so that in itself wasn't unusual. But he was always so deliberate about it. She'd often wondered if that was why she had these strange feelings for him, because she thought he really *saw* her.

He came to a stop in front of her. "Do you mind if I sit?"

She shrugged.

He sat, but didn't say anything more for a while. "Do you come out here at night a lot?" he finally asked.

"No."

"I didn't think so. I've walked around this track

at night all summer, and I've never seen you, like I do during the school year." She wondered why he walked the track at night. She was too nervous to ask. "Are you ready for school to start?"

She suddenly stood. Being this close to him made her heart feel lighter. He made her whole world seem lighter. But it was all a horrible illusion. "I've got to go."

"Where are you going?" he asked as she clomped down the bleachers in her heavy black boots.

"I don't know."

"I'll walk you," he said as he stood and followed her.

"No."

"I'm not going to let you walk alone at this time of night."

She stepped off the last bleacher and walked across the track to the football field. She looked over her shoulder. "Stop following me." Once she reached the middle of the field, she looked back again. "I said, stop following me."

"I'm not letting you walk alone."

That made her stop and turn to him. "What is the matter with you? Stop being so . . . so . . ."

"What?"

"Nice to me." She lowered herself to the ground and sat cross-legged. "I'm sitting here until you go away." This didn't exactly have the effect she wanted. "Don't sit beside me. Don't . . ." She

sighed when Sawyer sat beside her, right there on the fifty-yard line.

"What is the matter with you?" he asked.

She looked away. "My dad is sending me away to boarding school tomorrow."

"You're *leaving*?" he asked incredulously.

She nodded.

He pulled at some of the grassy turf around them. Finally he said, "Can I tell you something?"

"Not unless it's goodbye."

"Stop being such a smart-ass." That made her swing her head around. Her father and Beverly had been treading so lightly around her all summer that it was surprising to hear someone willing to call her on her attitude. "This past year, sometimes I would get up in the mornings and actually look forward to going to school because I knew I would see you. I would wonder what you were going to wear. I loved lunch because I could sit in the cafeteria and look out the window and see you up there on the bleachers. I've been looking for you all summer. Where have you been?"

Her mouth gaped and she felt like punching him on the arm. He had a girlfriend named Holly who, despite being in Dulcie Shelby's group Sassafras, was mostly nice. And they'd been going together forever. People even referred to them as a single entity. Sawyernholly. "What is *wrong* with you?" Julia said. "You and Holly belong together. You match."

"I'm just saying I'm sorry I never talked to you. I've always wanted to. I've always wanted . . ." His eyes went to her lips, and she was suddenly very aware of how close they were, of how he was leaning in toward her.

His lips were inches from hers when she turned away. "Go away, Sawyer. Go back to your nice, perfect life." She felt tears come to her eyes, and she wiped at them with the back of her hands. They came away streaked with her thick black eyeliner. The tears kept coming and she kept wiping her face, knowing she was making it worse. God, why didn't Sawyer just go and leave her to her ugly misery?

Sawyer very calmly took off his white polo shirt and handed it to her. "Go on. Use it."

She reluctantly took it and scrubbed her face with the shirt. It smelled like something green and fresh—like flower stems.

When she finally stopped crying, she looked at the shirt in her hands. She balled it up, embarrassed. She'd ruined it. "I'm sorry."

"I don't care about the shirt. Are you going to be okay?"

"I don't know." And her eyes started watering again. "I don't want to go away to school. But my dad doesn't want me anymore. He has *Beverly* now." The school had been Beverly's idea, of course. Why couldn't she have just kept her mouth shut about the cuts?

"I'm sure that's not true," Sawyer said.

She just shook her head. He didn't understand, after all.

He reached over to her and hesitantly pushed some of her crisp pink hair behind her ear. "I forgot what you looked like without makeup."

"I disappear."

"No. You're beautiful."

She didn't believe him. She *couldn't* believe him. "Go to hell, Sawyer."

"You can believe whatever you want. But I don't lie."

"Of course you don't. You're perfect." She paused, then turned to him. "You think I'm beautiful?"

"I've always thought that."

"What about these?" she said, drawing up the sleeves of the button-down she was wearing. She showed him the lines on her arms. Her father and Beverly had emptied her room of any sharp objects, like she was a toddler, so many of the deeper cuts were healed over, but she would still use her fingernails when she got anxious. "Do you think these are beautiful?"

Sawyer actually recoiled, which was exactly what she wanted him to do. It was proof. She really was unlovable. "Christ. Did you do that to yourself?"

She pulled the sleeves down. "Yes."

She expected him to leave her then, but he

didn't. They sat in silence for a long time. Finally she got tired and leaned back so that she was stretched out on the ground. He watched her, then slowly lowered himself back beside her.

The sky was incredible that night, the moon nearly full and the stars littering the sky like tossed stones. She'd never been away from Mullaby before. Would the sky look like this in Baltimore?

When Sawyer's stomach growled, he laughed. "I haven't had anything to eat since the cake I had for lunch," he said sheepishly.

"You had cake for lunch?"

"I'd have cake all the time if I could. You're going to laugh at this, but I'll tell you anyway. You know how some people have a sweet tooth? Well, I have a sweet *sense*. When I was a little boy, I could be playing across town and know exactly when my mother took a cake out of the oven. I could *see* the scent, how it floated through the air. All I had to do was follow it home. I will fiercely deny that if you ever say anything."

It was such a surprising thing to admit. She turned her head and saw that he was staring at her again. "You're charmed," she said. "But you probably know that already. It's even in the way you look at people." She stared at him for a moment, gorgeous and bare-chested in the moonlight. "Yes, you know exactly what power you have."

"Do I have a power over you?"

Did he honestly think she was immune? "Of course you do."

He lifted up on one elbow and looked down at her. What she wouldn't give to see what he saw, to know what made him look at her that way. "Can I kiss you, Julia?"

She didn't hesitate. "Yes."

She was confused when he carefully pushed her long-sleeved shirt off her shoulders. Even though she was wearing a tank top underneath, her arms were exposed. She squirmed and tried to cover them again, but then he did the most extraordinary thing.

He kissed her arms.

And she was done for.

He not only saw her, he accepted her. He wanted her. At that time in her life, at that moment, she couldn't think of any other person in the world who felt that way about her. Only him.

They made love that night, and stayed on the football field until dawn. He walked her home and they made promises to stay in touch, promises, it turned out, only one of them meant to keep. She left for Collier Reformatory in Maryland thinking she might be able to get through this, after all, because she now had Sawyer to come home to.

Looking back, she found that she could forgive him because it had been her fault for putting her happiness in the hands of someone else.

It had been so easy to do, though. He'd made her

feel true happiness for the first time in a long time that night. How could she not have succumbed to it?

But sometimes she wondered if she'd *lost* true happiness that night, as well.

And she'd been looking for it ever since.

Everywhere but here.

Chapter 6

*T*hat afternoon, with nothing better to do and no one to talk to—Grandpa Vance was holed up in his room again and Julia wasn't home— Emily started cleaning. She dusted until she looked like she was covered in hoary frost. She tackled her room first, cleaning everything but the chandelier because she couldn't find a ladder to get up to it, then she went to the other rooms, opening blinds and shedding light into corners that looked like they hadn't seen the sun in years. It was an adventure at first—apparently chasing the light last night had given her a taste for it— exploring the unknown, learning the story of the house. But she soon realized the story was a sad one. There was a room that had obviously once been a little boy's room. There were blue sailboats on the wallpaper and safety rails still on the bed. Maybe it had been Grandpa Vance's as a boy. Or did he have a brother? If so, what happened to him? Then there was a room with a bed that was twice as long as a normal one. There was a vanity table in the room, too, a feminine touch. Grandpa Vance had obviously shared this room with his wife. Where was his wife? Where were all the people who had once lived here?

She started to feel claustrophobic, overwhelmed by the history of this place. She wanted to feel a part of it, but her mother had told her nothing. *Nothing.* Why?

She went to the balcony outside her room for some fresh air. She kicked at the leaves, and decided to sweep them away. She swept until she had a large pile of leaves pushed against the balustrade. She set the broom aside and gathered some leaves in her arms, then tossed them over the side. They smelled mulchy and looked like someone had cut them out of craft paper. She scooped up some more and tossed them, stopping this time to watch the leaves fall. It wasn't until they hit the head of the person standing on the front porch steps that she had any idea someone was there.

"Julia!" she called. "Hi!"

Julia smiled up at her, leaves in her hair, and said, "Bored, are we?"

"I'm so glad you're here! I have something to tell you."

She ran downstairs and out the front door, thrilled that she had someone to discuss last night with. Julia was standing on the porch with two large brown paper bags in her arms and leaves still in her hair.

"I saw the light again last night!" Emily said excitedly. "It's not a ghost, Julia. I chased it, and it had *footsteps*."

This revelation didn't garner the reaction she'd wanted. Julia looked dismayed. "You *chased* it?"

"Yes."

"Emily, please don't do that," Julia said gently. "The Mullaby lights are harmless."

Before Emily could ask why Julia didn't think this was a huge discovery, the screen door squeaked behind her and Emily turned around to see Grandpa Vance duck under the doorway.

He'd changed clothes since she'd last seen him that morning, when she'd followed him to breakfast, like he had designated morning clothes and evening clothes. She'd hardly slept at all last night after chasing the light through the woods, and she'd been awake when she'd heard him leave. She'd intended to wait for him outside the restaurant and walk home with him again. But then Win had distracted her. She'd followed Win to a diner, where she'd watched him go in and vanish in the crowd. She'd gone home after that and waited for Grandpa Vance there, but when he'd gotten home, he'd disappeared into his room after leaving an egg sandwhich for her on the kitchen counter.

"Julia," he said. "I thought I heard your voice."

"I brought you a gift." Julia handed the bags she was holding up to Vance, who looked like he'd been given the Holy Grail of foodstuffs. "With this heat, I thought cooking dinner would be the last thing either of you wanted to do today. Maybe the two of you could eat together," she said with a significance that wasn't lost on Emily. She was trying to get them to spend some time together. Emily appreciated the effort, but didn't think it would do much good.

But Grandpa Vance nosed around in the bags and surprised her with his zeal. "You're in for a treat, Emily! Julia's barbecue is the best in town. It's all because of her smokehouse. Electric smokers just aren't the same. My mouth is watering already. Will you join us, Julia?"

"No, thanks. I have to be going."

"You're right neighborly. Thank you." Vance disappeared inside, leaving Emily on the porch with Julia.

"That's the first time he's been out of his room since this morning," Emily said, amazed.

"Barbecue gets him every time."

"I'll remember that."

"Listen," Julia said, "how would you like to go to Piney Woods Lake with me on Saturday? It's *the* place for kids your age to go in the summer. Maybe you can meet some people you'll be going to school with."

It felt nice to be included. Those elderly ladies

this morning had to be wrong. She could fit in here. "Okay. Sure."

"Great. See you tomorrow. Now go talk with your grandfather." Without another word about the lights, Julia gave her a backward wave and jogged down the front porch steps.

Emily turned and went back into the house. She thought about just going to her room and letting Grandpa Vance eat in peace, but then she decided to give it one more try. When she reached the kitchen, she heard the dryer door close and Vance came out of the attached laundry room. He'd been looking in the clothes dryer again. He was inordinately preoccupied with it, which was strange because just that afternoon, someone from the dry cleaner's had come by to take a bag of laundry he'd left on the porch.

Vance stopped when he saw her. "Emily." He cleared his throat. "So, um, has the wallpaper in your bedroom changed yet?"

"Changed?" she asked.

"It does that sometimes. Changes on its own."

It sounded like something you would say to a child. The moon is made of cheese. Wish on a star. There's magic wallpaper in your room. He probably thought of her as a little girl, she realized, and he was trying to make her smile. "No, it's still lilacs. But I'll be on the lookout," she said to humor him.

He nodded seriously. "All right, then."

In the silence that followed, Emily looked around and found where he had set the bags on the table in the breakfast nook. "Are you going to eat now?" she finally asked.

"I thought I might," he said. "Would you like to join me?"

"You wouldn't mind?"

"Not at all. Have a seat." He took plates and utensils out of the cabinets and put them on the table. They sat opposite each other, and together they unloaded the contents of the bags, mostly Styrofoam containers of various sizes, plus a few hamburger buns and two slices of cake.

Vance took the lids off all the containers. His incredibly long fingers were clumsy and his hands shook a little.

"What is this?" Emily asked, looking in the largest Styrofoam container. There was a bunch of dry-looking chopped meat inside.

"Barbecue."

"This isn't barbecue," Emily said. "Barbecue is hot dogs and hamburgers on a grill."

Vance laughed, which automatically made Emily smile. "Ha! Blasphemy! In North Carolina, barbecue means *pork,* child. Hot dogs and hamburgers on a grill—that's called 'cooking out' around here," he explained with sudden enthusiasm. "And there are two types of North Carolina barbecue sauce—Lexington and Eastern North Carolina. Here, look." He excitedly found a container of sauce and showed her, accidentally spilling some on the table. "Lexington-style is the sweet sugar-and-tomato-based sauce, some people call it the red sauce, that you put on chopped or pulled pork shoulder. Julia's restaurant is Lexington-style. But there are plenty of Eastern North Carolina–style restaurants here. They use a thin, tart, vinegar-and-pepper-based sauce. And, generally, they use the whole hog. But no matter the style, there's always hush puppies and coleslaw. And, if I'm not mistaken, those are slices of Milky Way cake. Julia makes the best Milky Way cakes."

"Like the candy bar?"

"Yep. The candy bars are melted and poured into the batter. It means 'Welcome.' "

Emily looked over to the cake Julia had brought yesterday morning, still on the counter. "I thought an apple stack cake meant 'Welcome.' "

"Any kind of cake means 'Welcome,' " he said. "Well, except for coconut cake. You give coconut cake and fried chicken when there's a death."

Emily looked at him strangely.

"And occasionally a broccoli casserole," he added.

Emily watched as Vance picked up the container of barbecue and forked some chopped pork onto the bottom hamburger bun. He poured some sauce on it, then topped it with coleslaw. He capped it all with the top bun and handed it on a plate to Emily. "A barbecue sandwich, North Carolina–style."

"Thank you," Emily said, smiling as she took the strange sandwich. He really was a nice man. She liked being around him. And he made her feel so small, like there was so much more to the world than just her problems, her grief. "This was nice of Julia to do."

"Julia is a wonderful person. Her father would have been very proud of her."

"I was just talking to her about the Mullaby lights," Emily said, hoping he'd be more interested in what she'd discovered than Julia had been. "I've been seeing them at night."

Vance paused in the middle of handing her the container of hush puppies. "You have? Where?"

"In the woods behind the house," she said as she reached over and took the container from him.

"I'll only ask you to do one thing while you're here, Emily," he said seriously. "Just one. Stay away from them."

"But I don't think it's a ghost," she said. "I think someone is doing it on purpose."

"No one is doing it on purpose. Trust me."

She wasn't usually an argumentative person, despite her mother's love of passionate debates. But Emily had to bite her tongue to keep from pointing out that leaving her a box of Band-Aids last night seemed pretty intentional.

"Your mother would get that same look on her face when she was a little girl," he said. "She was stubborn, my Dulcie." He hastily looked away, as if he'd said too much. Suddenly that old awkward tension was back, joining them at the table with apologies for being so late.

Emily toyed with the hush puppies on her plate. "Why don't you want to talk about her?"

Still not looking at her, he said, "I get all confused about it. I don't know what to say."

Emily nodded, though she didn't really understand. Maybe, like everything else about him, his grief was larger than anyone's, so big that no one could see around it. Vance's relationship with his daughter must have been a complicated one. But then, her mother's relationship with everyone had been complicated. She'd been a hard woman to know. High-spirited and mercurial, she'd been like the mist from perfume. You had to be content to let a little of it sprinkle over you. And then, eventually, it went away.

She wouldn't push him. And she would try not to be hurt by his avoidance. He'd taken her in when she had no other place to go, after all, and she was grateful. So she would talk to other people in town about her mother, find out more from them. Maybe she could find other members of Sassafras. Maybe she'd even see Win Coffey again and ask him about the relationship his uncle had had with her mother. He'd said next time he saw her he'd tell her about their history.

She liked that thought. Seeing Win again.

They ate in silence. Afterward, Grandpa Vance again checked the clothes dryer, as if something might have appeared during dinner. But again he found nothing, so he went to his room. Emily went upstairs and finished sweeping, then she sat on the balcony and waited for the lights.

And so ended her second full day in Mullaby.

LATER THAT evening, when Vance ducked out of his room to check the dryer one last time before bed, he paused to look up the staircase. He didn't hear any more shuffling. No more scraping of a broom. Emily had settled in for the night.

It was a peculiar thing, he thought, having someone in the house again. He'd almost forgotten what it was like. Emily made the air different, vibrating, as if there were music close by but he couldn't quite hear it. He was surprised by how much fuller he felt with her near, and he didn't know how to handle it. Being needed was a lot like being tall—it was never really an issue until other people were around.

Vance had towered over all the other kids in kindergarten. That was his first memory of truly understanding how tall he was. Up until then, while he was certainly big for his age, he was still the shortest member of his own normal-sized family. Some kids in school teased him at first, but there a came a point when they realized that maybe it wasn't the best idea to pick a fight with someone who could knock them over with only the wind he caused by walking past them.

His family was gone now. Vance was the only one left of the Shelbys, and he had inherited the existing fortune. He knew he wasn't supposed to have it all. It wasn't supposed to all come down to him—the Shelby legacy, the Shelby name. There were supposed to be brothers and sisters who would do great things. There were supposed to be normal kids in his family. For a while there were. But his older sister, for whom the wallpaper in her room was always pink candy swirls, drowned in Piney Woods Lake when she was eleven. And then there was his younger brother, who died from a fall out of the tree house in the front yard when he was six. His parents tried for more children after that, but to no avail. They were stuck with Vance. Vance, who was so tall his feet reached the bottom of the lake, so he could never drown, and his arms reached all the way to the limbs in the trees, so he never had to climb and fall.

His parents died when he was in his twenties. He thought he saw disappointment in their faces when they passed away. Their legacy, it was all going to the giant. What was Vance going to do with it? they probably thought. He'd never get married. Who would want him?

He was thirty-two and living alone, rarely venturing outside, when he met Lily. She was related to the Sullivans down the street and, while attending State, came to visit them one weekend. If she'd been a color, she would have been bright green. If she'd been a scent, she would have been new paper. She was happy and intelligent and afraid of nothing. The Sullivan boys, who had taken to throwing balls into Vance's yard and daring each other to fetch them and risk getting eaten by the Giant of Mullaby, had shared this story with their cousin. Lily was appalled. She took them by their ears and forced them into the yard and up the front porch steps, determined to get them to apologize. When Vance came to the door, Lily was so stunned that she let go of the boys. They instantly ran away. A few hours later, when Lily hadn't returned home, they cried to their mother that the Giant of Mullaby had eaten her. When their mother went to investigate, she found Lily and Vance sitting on the front porch steps, drinking iced tea and laughing. She'd paused, then backed away. Something wonderful was happening and she could see it right away. No one had ever made Vance laugh like that.

Vance and Lily married after Lily graduated, and Lily taught second grade at Mullaby Elementary until she became pregnant with Dulcie. Those were halcyon days. Lily didn't let him stay in the house. She insisted they go grocery shopping together, go to the movie theater, attend Little League games. People had always been curious about him, but that was only because he used to hide. Once he left the house, he came to realize that Mullaby easily accepted him. He was, in a town full of strange things, just another oddity. Vance was so grateful for this revelation that he helped fund playgrounds and war memorials and scholarships.

He almost died himself when Lily passed away. Dulcie was twelve when it happened. It was like snow had settled over their world, turning everything cold and silent. It was only Vance's memory of Lily's bright greenness, of her joy and intelligence, of her strong faith in everything, but especially in him, that made him survive. How Dulcie got through it, he had no idea. And that was one of his biggest shames.

Vance thought a person could only bear going through that once in a lifetime.

Then he learned that his daughter had died.

When Dulcie's friend Merry called and told him that Dulcie had been in a car accident, Vance couldn't even speak. He hung up the phone and crawled upstairs to Dulcie's old room, but then he couldn't get back down, so he stayed up there a week, the wallpaper in her bedroom turning gray and wet, like storm clouds. He wanted to die. What reason was there to go on? Everything that had tethered him to this world was now gone.

When Julia next door finally got to him, he hadn't eaten in so long he couldn't walk. He spent a week in the hospital, where his legs dangled off the end of the bed and it took three sheets to cover him.

After he got home from the hospital, there were several phone messages left by Merry. Dulcie had a daughter, she said. And she needed a place to live. Merry couldn't keep her because she was moving back to her home in Canada. She'd hired a private detective to try to find any close relatives on both Emily's mother's and father's sides. And Vance was it.

He'd always taken a passive stance in life. He knew that. His height made him shy. His parents had left him a fortune. His wife had found *him*. Lily had always taken care of everything. And Dulcie had basically been on her own since she was twelve. Now it was his turn. He finally had to step up and take care of something.

He hadn't done a very good job of taking care of Emily so far. Dulcie hadn't told Emily anything about Mullaby, about what had happened, so Vance was terrified of saying something Dulcie wouldn't want her daughter to know. When Dulcie left, she'd sworn him to secrecy. *Don't speak of it,* she'd said. *And maybe it will go away. Maybe one day everyone will forget.* He'd let his daughter down in countless ways, so he'd been determined to keep his word about this. And he had, for twenty years. Now he didn't know what to do. Emily had attracted the attention of the Mullaby lights already. She was going to want answers.

He walked to the kitchen in the darkness. But instead of going into the laundry room to check the dryer, he went directly to the back door and opened it. Sure enough, like Emily said, there was a light in the woods in the backyard, not moving, as if watching the house.

Vance stepped onto the porch, making himself seen. The light immediately disappeared. He heard a gasp, then footsteps on the balcony above. He stepped off the low kitchen porch and looked up.

Emily was standing there, staring out into the woods.

She didn't see him, so he quietly moved away.

He'd made this mistake once.

He wasn't going to again.

Chapter 7

Piney Woods Lake was exactly that—a lake in the middle of a thick nest of pine trees. It looked like water in a deep blue bowl, like it could be accidentally tipped out and poured into the surrounding countryside. Julia parked her old black Ford truck, which had belonged to her father, in one of the last spaces in the crowded parking lot above the boardwalk. It had been a long time since she'd been out here. The last time was probably with her father, pre-Beverly. She'd forgotten how beautiful it was. When she and Emily got out, they were assaulted by a cacophony of summertime scents and sounds. Wet sand, coconut oil, boat motors, kids laughing, music playing.

"It's so loud!" Emily said. "I like it already."

"Your mother liked it out here, too, as I recall. I remember hearing about a place in the cove where Sassafras would meet and rule over the beach all summer," she said as she swung her beach bag over her shoulder and led Emily across the hot, gummy parking lot.

They walked down to the boardwalk, and from there to the beach. Because of the crowds, they had to walk in single file. Julia kept looking back to see if Emily was keeping up. Emily smiled the entire way, stopping to take off her shoes, then running to catch up.

They finally stopped at a place halfway between the boardwalk and the cove. There were houses above the beach on this end of the lake, large houses with glass walls overlooking the glittery blue water. As Julia took two towels out of her bag and spread them on the sand, Emily shaded her eyes from the glare of sun and looked around. "Were you meeting Sawyer here?"

"No. Why?" Julia asked as she shimmied out of her white shorts, revealing the bottom half of her red bikini. She left her gauzy long-sleeved shirt on over her red bikini top, though.

"Because he's coming this way."

Julia immediately turned to see him walking down the beach toward them. Sawyer stood out too much to blend in anywhere, but the closest he came was here, with the sun and the sand. He was golden. A sun king.

"He's nice," Emily said wistfully. "The moment I saw him, I knew he'd have an accent like that. I don't know why."

"Some men you know are Southern before they ever say a word," Julia said as she and Emily watched Sawyer's progress, helpless, almost as if they couldn't look away. "They remind you of something good—picnics or carrying sparklers around at night. Southern men will hold doors open for you, they'll hold you after you yell at them, and they'll hold on to their pride no matter what. Be careful what they tell you, though. They have a way of making you believe anything, because they say it *that way*."

"What way?" Emily asked as she turned to her, intrigued.

"I hope you never find out," she said.

"You've been spoken to *that way*?"

"Yes," she said softly, just as Sawyer stopped at their towels.

"Hello, ladies."

"Hi, Sawyer," Emily said as she sat down.

Julia sat on the towel next to her and stuffed her shorts into her beach bag. "What are you doing here?"

"Oh, I don't know, Julia," he said. "Bear hunting?"

She squinted up at him. "Is that a euphemism for something?"

He ignored that and sat on her towel at her feet. She could see her reflection in his sunglasses as he stared at her. What was he doing? Why was he being so familiar? The eighteen years of silence while she was gone, along with the year and a half of cold shoulder she'd given him since she'd been back, should have been more than enough to discourage him from sitting on her towel on the beach, inches away from her bare legs.

Yet here he was.

And all because she'd told Stella that she made cakes because of him.

Stupid, stupid, stupid.

"My sister is in town for the weekend," he said. "She and her daughter are staying at the family's lake house. I came to see them."

"So this has nothing to do with my telling you I was taking Emily out here today?" she asked skeptically.

"Now, that would be too easy, wouldn't it?"

"Everything is easy for you, Sawyer."

"Not everything." Before she had a chance to respond, he nudged his chin in the direction behind her. "There's my niece. Ingrid!" he called.

Julia and Emily turned to see a pretty redheaded teenager change course and walk over to them. Julia seemed to remember Sawyer's older sister having red hair.

"This is Julia Winterson," he said to his niece.

Ingrid smiled. "I recognize the pink streak in your hair. I see you sometimes in town when my mom and I visit," she said. "I love it, by the way."

"Thanks," Julia said. "This is Emily. She just moved here."

"Some kids over in the cove are having a cookout party and they asked me if I wanted to come. I'm going to ask my mom. Do you want to come, Emily?" Ingrid asked.

Emily looked at her blankly. "What is it for?"

"What do you mean?"

"Is it a club?"

"It's a party," Ingrid said, giving Emily a questioning look as she turned to leave. "I'll be right back."

Emily still looked confused.

"You're making this out to be harder than it really is," Julia said, laughing as she patted Emily's hand. "All you have to say is 'I'd love to come!'"

"Like this," Sawyer said. "Julia, would you like to go out with me Monday night?"

"I'd love to!" she playacted. "See? Easy. It's just a party. Didn't you go to parties at your old school?"

"Well, I helped organize parties with my mom. Usually fundraisers. And some community service clubs at school used to have end-of-the-year parties."

"What kind of school did you go to?"

"Roxley School for Girls. My mom helped found it. It's a school based on social activism and global awareness. Volunteering is part of the curriculum."

There again was that hint that Dulcie might have done some good with her life. Emily had mentioned something about it before, about Dulcie and her causes. As unbelievable as it seemed, Dulcie must have changed when she left here. "Well, there's no reason for this party. It's just for fun."

Emily gave her a dubious look.

Julia laughed again. "You'll be fine. I'll be right here when you want to go home. No pressure."

Ingrid came back shortly and said, "Are you ready, Emily?"

Emily stood, put on a smile Julia was sure she didn't mean, and walked away with Ingrid.

"Who would have thought Dulcie would have raised such a decent girl?" Sawyer said.

"She is a nice kid, isn't she?"

"You're good with her. And no, I'm not surprised."

Julia shrugged uneasily, realizing she was alone with him now and she couldn't run away from what she knew he wanted to talk about. "I figure she needs someone she can turn to until she gets settled. I remember what it was like being that age. And believe me, I'm profoundly grateful to be on this side of it now."

Sawyer was quiet for a moment as he studied her. She wished he would take off his sunglasses. She didn't like seeing how uncomfortable she looked.

It was natural, she supposed, to be tense around him. Your peers when you're a teenager will always be the keepers of your embarrassment and regret. It was one of life's great injustices, that you can move on and be accomplished and happy, but the moment you see someone from high school you immediately become the person you were then, not the person you are now. When she was around Sawyer, she was the old Julia—the messed-up daughter of a man who hadn't finished high school and cooked barbecue for a living. Sawyer never did anything to make her feel that way, but it inevitably happened. She could blame a lot of things on him, but not that.

"Why don't you take off your shirt?" he finally asked.

"I bet you say that to all the girls." When he didn't respond, she said, "You know why." She reached over to her beach bag for a bottle of water, but Sawyer caught her arm.

He held her arm and slowly pushed the sleeve up. It took great effort not to snatch her arm away. She had to remind herself that he'd seen them before. Most people had. She couldn't hide them all the time.

He trailed his thumb over the scars. Some were as thin as wire, others were thick and raised. It was a surprisingly tender thing to do and it made her heart ache, just a little.

"Who did you turn to when you were her age, Julia?"

You. "No one. That's how I know." She slid her arm out of his grasp. "I don't like to get sun on them. A tan makes them look worse."

"Did you ever feel like you could turn to your dad or your stepmother?"

"Dad didn't know what to do with me. And Beverly considered her job taking care of Dad, not being a mother to me. But she was the one who convinced him to send me away to school. I'll always be grateful for that. Leaving this place probably saved my life."

"And you can't wait to leave again," he said.

"Six months and counting."

He sprawled out on his side in front of her, his head propped on his hand. "So, what time should I pick you up?"

"Pick me up for what?" she said as she found her bottle of water and took a sip.

"For our date on Monday. You accepted my invitation. I have a witness."

She snorted. "Don't be ridiculous."

"I'm serious."

"No, you're not. Go coax the shirt off someone else. Your charm doesn't work on me. I have a force field deflecting it."

"Please. You'd have no idea what to do if I turned it on full blast."

"You're not scaring me."

"Yes, I am. And that's why I'm stopping. I want to talk about it, Julia," he said. "But not now." He rolled onto his back, the golden hairs on his legs and arms sparkling like spun sugar.

"You don't get to decide that," she told him. He didn't respond. She waited for him to go away, but he didn't. He might have even fallen asleep.

She took a book out of her bag and moved as far away from him as she could, wondering what pitiful part of her heart actually enjoyed this, his nearness.

The part that would always be sixteen years old, she supposed, frozen forever before everything changed.

THE CLOSER they got to the party, the more nervous Emily became. She wouldn't have thought twice about it if it hadn't been for those old ladies. Now she was worried about what everyone would think of her. She kept telling herself that there was no reason why she shouldn't fit in. She just had a temporary case of new-girl-itis.

The group was assembled away from the beach, in a small grotto formed by the trees at the back of the cove. Music was playing. Some kids were holding drinks in plastic cups. A couple of guys were playing touch football and getting in everyone's way. There were a few adults there, one of whom was manning the grill and seemed to be master of ceremonies. He was a large, gregarious man with black hair and a booming voice.

Once they got into the thick of things, Ingrid left her alone. Emily walked to the periphery of the party, toward the back of the grotto by the trees. She took a few deep breaths. No reason to panic.

Julia said this was where Sassafras had gathered in the summer. Emily could tell that it had been a popular spot for kids for quite some time, because the tree trunks were covered with carvings of names and initials. One carving in particular caught her eye. It was a large heart with the initials D.S. + L.C. inside. She wondered if the D.S. stood for Dulcie Shelby. That made her smile. It was nice to imagine a boy who had once loved her mother so much that he'd carved their initials into a tree. Her mother hadn't dated much in her adult life. The few dates she did have were with men she'd met through her work, and they'd all been brief flings. She'd never wanted anything serious. She'd been very open about that with Emily. *Always make your needs and expectations known,* she used to say. *That way no one gets hurt.* As far as Emily could tell, the only serious relationship her mother ever had was with Emily's father, and even it hadn't started out that way. They'd met during a high-seas standoff with fishermen over the killing of dolphins. They'd spent ten days on a boat together, and Emily had been the result. Her father had died in a Sea Shepherd boating accident two years later, trying to stop illegal whaling. Her mother and father had never married and Emily had no memory of him, so he was like most things in her mother's past, mysterious and unmentionable.

As she was standing there staring at the tree, her back to the party, she suddenly felt something odd, like ribbons of warmth wrapping around her from behind. It was alarming, and she wanted to fight it at first, to fling her arms and shake whatever it was off. But she stopped herself because she didn't want to look idiotic in front of all these kids. She waited it out and realized that it didn't feel bad. Not at all. She closed her eyes and felt almost . . . comforted.

She opened her eyes again, and something made her turn around.

There was Win Coffey.

He had on long swim trunks, which were dark with water and sticking to his thighs. His hair was wet and dripping into his eyes, and he smelled like warm lake water.

She cleared her throat. "I almost didn't recognize you without your suit," she said.

A corner of his mouth lifted, amused. "It's a different kind of suit."

"But no bow tie."

"Hard to swim in. I've tried."

Her eyes went from his lips to his chin, then to the rivulets of water running down his bare chest. Embarrassed, she quickly met his eyes again. It looked as if he'd come right out of the water and made a beeline for her. But how could he have known she was there? How could he have seen her from the water? Over his shoulder, she could see that some kids were watching them and whispering to each other. Win didn't seem to care. He clearly fit in. It had to count for something, his interest in her. "Do all these kids go to the same school?" she asked.

"Some are summer lake residents who leave in the fall," he said, not taking his eyes off her. "Some are permanent residents who, yes, go to school here."

"Mullaby High?"

"Yes."

"I'll be a senior there in the fall."

"I know. I will, too." He ran both his hands through his dark wet hair, slicking it back. It almost made her breath catch. "Not that it isn't nice to see you again, but I have to ask: What are you doing here?"

"Here?" she asked. "You mean at this party?"

"Yes."

"Trying to blend in."

"It's not working. Prepare yourself."

"For what?" And no sooner did she ask than a dark-haired girl in an orange bathing suit came to a stop beside Win.

"You're Emily Benedict, aren't you?" she asked, with the same combination of aversion and curiosity Win had had the first day she'd met him, but with a little more bite.

"Yes," Win said before Emily could. "Emily, this is my sister, Kylie."

"You weren't invited," Kylie said bluntly. "You're going to ruin my party."

"I . . . I came with Ingrid," Emily said, feeling a hot prickle of embarrassment.

"You should leave."

Win finally took his eyes off Emily to give a look of censure to his sister. "Kylie, stop being rude."

"I'm not being rude. I'm serious. She should leave." Kylie pointed over her shoulder. Win turned to see that the big man, the master of ceremonies, had left the grill and was slowly making his way toward them.

Win cursed. "Let's go." He took Emily by the arm and together they skirted the party, following the tree line. When they reached the regular part of the beach, Win stopped once they were out of sight of the grotto.

She rubbed her arm where he'd held it. The place where he'd touched her felt warm. "I'm sorry," she said, a little taken aback at how fast that had happened. "I didn't know it was a private party."

They faced each other on the crowded beach, hot summer noise humming around them. "It's not."

It took a moment to sink in. It wasn't a private party. That meant *she* wasn't welcome. Just her. "Oh."

"Has your grandfather told you yet?" Win asked, seemingly out of the blue.

"Told me what?"

"About your mother and my uncle. That's what that was all about." He nudged his chin back toward the grotto.

Confused as to why being kicked out of the party had anything to do with her mother and his uncle, she said, "Actually, I was hoping to run into you again so I could ask. You said next time I saw you you'd tell me."

"I did say that, didn't I? 'Next time' seemed so far away." Win hesitated before he said, "My uncle committed suicide when he was a teenager."

She wasn't expecting that, and didn't know how to respond. The best she could come up with was "I'm sorry."

"He did it because of your mother."

She felt a jolt of alarm. She suddenly thought of the initials on the tree. D.S. + L.C.

Dulcie Shelby and Logan Coffey.

"They were in love," Win said, watching her closely. "Or, he was in love with her. His family didn't want him to be with her, but he went against their wishes, against years of tradition. Then your mother turned around and broke his heart, like what he did, what he sacrificed, didn't matter."

Emily was desperately trying to make sense of this. "Hold on. Are you saying you blame my mother for his death?"

"Everyone blames her, Emily."

"What do you mean, *everyone?*" She could hear her voice rising.

Win noticed, too. He adjusted the waistband of his swim trunks, then settled his hands on his lean hips. "I'm sorry. I should have thought how to say that in a nicer way. This is a little harder than I thought it would be."

"Than you thought *what* would be?" she demanded. "Convincing me that my mother was responsible for your uncle's suicide? I have news for you, my mother was a wonderful person. She would never do anything if she thought it was going to hurt another person. Never."

Win suddenly looked over his shoulder, as if sensing something about to happen. "My dad is still looking for me. Come this way." He took her hand and led her away from the water, toward the pine trees.

Her bare feet kicked up sand as she jogged to keep up with him. "Where are we going?"

"Out of sight," he said, the moment she stepped onto the cool, pine-needle floor. The smell of rosin was strong. It reminded her of Christmas wreaths and red glass ornaments. It was a completely different world, a completely different season, than just a few steps away at the lake.

"I don't have shoes on," she said, pulling him to a stop.

He turned to her. "You seem to find yourself without shoes in the woods a lot."

She wasn't amused. "Why are you doing this?"

"Believe it or not, I'm trying to help you."

"Help me do what?" She threw her hands in the air, frustrated.

"Adjust."

She scoffed at him, because if adjusting to this place meant believing what he said about her mother, she was *never* going to adjust.

Before she could turn to go back to the beach, he said, "Okay, here are the basics. Your mother was known to be spoiled and cruel. My uncle was gullible and shy. She used his feelings for her to trick him into revealing a long-held Coffey family secret to the entire town, just because she could. Then she turned her back on him. Devastated that he'd lost her and hurt his family, he killed himself. She left town without so much as an apology. I know it's hard to hear. But this might go a long way in explaining why people here act . . . a certain way around you."

"Act what way?"

His dark, arched brows rose. "You haven't noticed yet?"

Emily hesitated.

"You *have* noticed."

She shook her head. She was angry at him for saying these things, but she was even angrier at herself for actually standing there and listening.

"You didn't know my mother. *I* knew my mother. She would never turn her back on anyone."

Win's eyes went soft and sympathetic. It was clear he was sorry she was hurt by his words, but he didn't look sorry that he'd said them in the first place. *This* was what he meant by the two of them having history?

"Why should I trust you, anyway?" she challenged him. "Why should I believe anything you say?"

He shrugged. "You probably shouldn't. You probably shouldn't have anything to do with me. I'm surprised your grandfather hasn't told you to stay away from me already. He will soon, though. Mark my words."

The wind picked up for a moment, brushing the treetops. A cascade of pine needles, both green and brown, suddenly fell down around them. Emily watched Win through the swarming needles, a peculiar enchantment coming over her. Who was this strange boy? What did he want from her?

"What secret did your uncle reveal?" she found herself asking.

He took a long time to answer, as if warring with himself. His lips finally lifted into a cynical smile, breaking the spell. "You wouldn't believe me if I told you."

He gladly shared some secrets, yet he wouldn't reveal his own. She should have no trouble casting aside anything someone so disingenuous would say. But still it lingered in her mind. And that made her furious.

She turned stiffly and walked back to the lake. Back to summer.

She made her way across the beach to where Julia was sitting cross-legged on her towel, reading a book. Sawyer was stretched out at her feet like a large marmalade cat.

Julia looked up when Emily's shadow fell over her. "Emily? What's wrong?" she asked, setting her book aside.

"Nothing. I'd like to go home, if that's okay." She suddenly, desperately, wanted to talk to her grandfather. He was her one true connection to her mother. He would tell her that what Win said was a lie.

Sawyer sat up. He took off his sunglasses. "You look upset," he said.

"I'm fine." She tacked on a smile for good measure.

"My sister was rude to her. I apologize." Win's voice behind her made her turn. She wasn't aware that he'd been following her. He met her eyes, his expression troubled.

Sawyer stood. For someone so beautiful, he could certainly be imposing when he got angry. He was as tall as Win, but much bigger. "What did she say that upset Emily?"

Before Win could answer, Julia said, "That was *your* party?"

"My sister's birthday party."

"Jesus," she said, grabbing her bag and quickly stuffing it with their towels, her book, and her water bottle. She stood. "I didn't know. Come on, sweetheart. Let's go home."

"I can take her," Win said. "It's on my way, and I need to be home before sunset anyway." He held out his hand and, without thinking, Emily took it. She immediately came to her senses and tried to take it back, but he held firm. His hand was warm and dry, like he'd just taken off a glove.

"I'm taking her home," Julia said.

"It would be no trouble."

Sawyer took a step forward. "I don't think that's a good idea, Win."

Win stared at Emily for a moment before saying, "That does seem to be the consensus." He finally let go of her hand. She missed the contact. It was crazy.

Julia put her arm around her and led her away. "Come on."

"Do you need me to go with you?" Sawyer called after them.

"No." Julia paused, looking back at him. Then she added, "But thanks."

Julia and Emily walked across the beach and to the parking lot in silence. When they climbed into the truck, the black seats hot from the sun, Julia immediately put the key in the ignition. As much as Emily didn't want to believe it, Julia's reaction was giving some credence to what Win had told her.

"Win said his uncle committed suicide because of my mother," Emily blurted out.

Julia started the engine. She obviously didn't want to comment.

"That's not true, is it?"

"Whether it's true or not, he shouldn't have told you," Julia said, turning to her and touching her arm.

Emily almost came undone. She liked the maternal way Julia treated her, but it was just too much right now. "He said she was cruel," she said, taking her hand away.

That made Julia wince a little. "This is something your grandfather has to tell you. Not me. And certainly not Win." Julia stared at her a moment, her sympathy, her genuine desire to make things all better, clear in her every pore. "It took me a long time to realize this: We get to choose what defines us. It doesn't make a lot of sense right now, but it will. Okay?"

Emily reluctantly nodded.

"All right, then." Julia put the truck in reverse. "I'll take you home to talk to your grandfather."

Chapter 8

Good, you're home," Grandpa Vance said as he ducked out of his room as soon as Emily came in the front door. She was surprised he'd come out on his own. She'd been prepared to smoke him out. "I was thinking, you need a car so you can go out to the lake whenever you want to, instead of being cooped up here. I happen to have one, you know. A car, I mean."

"Grandpa Vance—"

"I don't actually drive it. I've never been able to drive. Not with these legs. But your grandmother had a car. Come, I'll show you."

What was this all about? Just last night they were eating barbecue in silence. He led her through the kitchen, where he had to turn sideways because his shoulders were broader than the width of the doorway to the porch. She followed him out and around the side of the house. There was an old garage there that looked like it hadn't been used, or even opened, in ages. The driveway from the street no longer existed, so the garage stood in the grassy side yard like an island that had lost its mainland bridge.

When Vance pulled the garage door up, dust motes sparkled in the sunlight, but they couldn't see very far inside. He reached around and felt for the light switch. The fluorescent light popped on reluctantly, buzzing and flickering and complaining until it finally decided to shine properly on the car.

"It's a 1978 Oldsmobile Cutlass," he said. "Under all that dust, it's actually brown. If you wouldn't mind driving something this old, I'll have someone look it over."

Emily stared at it. "Did my mom used to drive this?"

"No. When she turned sixteen, she wanted a convertible, so I bought her one." He paused. "If you want something different, I can arrange that."

"No," she said immediately. "I think I like this one. It looks like a muscle car."

"A muscle car, huh? Lily would have liked that."

She turned to him. "Who is Lily?"

Vance looked shocked. "Lily was my wife, child," he said. "Did your mother never talk about her?"

"She didn't tell me anything." Emily tucked her hair behind her ears. *Talk to him.* "Grandpa Vance, today at the lake, there was this party. It turned out to be a party thrown by the Coffeys, and I was asked to leave."

If indignation were something you could see, it would look exactly like an eight-foot man pulling himself to his full height. *"You were asked to leave?"*

"Well, not in so many words," she said, still embarrassed by it. "But it was clear enough that the Coffeys don't like me. Well, except for Win. I think. Actually, I'm not really sure about him."

"That was the one thing I asked you to do, Emily!" he said. "To stay away from them."

Win was right. He said Grandpa Vance would soon tell her that. "You asked me to stay away from the Mullaby lights, not to stay away from the Coffeys. I didn't know I was doing anything wrong."

Vance took a deep breath and shook his head. "You're right. None of this is your fault." He looked at the car for a long moment before turning off the light. "I had hoped, with all the time that had passed, these old wounds had healed."

"Is this because of my mom?" she asked hesitantly. "Win told me some pretty unbelievable things today. He said she was cruel. But that can't be true. Mom was a wonderful person. Wasn't she a wonderful person? I know you don't want to talk about her. But please, just tell me that."

"Dulcie was a handful when she was a young girl," he said as he pulled the garage door down. "She was so stubborn and high-spirited. She could actually sting people with her energy. But she was also bright and happy and curious. She got that from Lily. Dulcie was twelve when Lily died." He looked away and rubbed his eyes with an embarrassed flick of his hand. "I didn't know how to handle her on my own. The only thing I could think to do was give her everything she asked for. She tested me at first, asking me for outrageous things, just to see how far I would go. But I never said no. So she got the best of everything. As she got older, she began to take great pleasure in teasing people who didn't have as much as she did. She *could* be very cruel sometimes. Julia was a frequent target."

Emily felt like she'd been walking upstairs and had suddenly missed a step. "My mom was cruel to Julia?"

He nodded slowly. "And others," he added reluctantly.

Emily could feel herself resisting this, wanting to push it away. This couldn't be her mother he was talking about. Her mother had been a good person, a selfless person. She'd wanted to save the world.

"She was the queen bee of her social circle, and her word was law. She had an incredible power over them. Who she accepted, they accepted. Who she shunned, they shunned," he said. "So when she took this shy, troubled boy named Logan Coffey under her wing and told everyone to accept him, they did."

"Win said he committed suicide."

"Yes."

Emily paused, wondering if she really wanted to ask what she was about to ask. "Did my mom have something to do with it?"

She waited, holding her breath, until he finally answered. "Yes."

"What did she do?" she whispered.

Vance seemed to struggle with what to say. He looked up at the sky for a moment, then said, "What did Win tell you?"

"He said Logan loved my mom, but his family didn't approve of her. He said Logan broke tradition to be with her, but all my mom wanted was to trick him into revealing a Coffey family secret."

Vance sighed. "The Coffeys are much more social these days, but you have to understand, back then they were very exclusive. Status was important to Dulcie. It started with me, giving her everything she wanted. It all got wrapped up in her grief over losing her mother. If only she had more, then she'd be happy. When the Coffeys wouldn't let her into their social circle, when they frowned on her relationship with Logan, it made her angry. Not just angry. Livid. She had a hard time with her temper after Lily died. She lashed out a lot. The Coffeys had, and still have, one particular quirk: They never come out at night. Never. But Logan came out at night for Dulcie. She assembled most of the town in front of the bandstand in the park one night, saying she was going to perform for them. She had a lovely singing voice. Instead, she led Logan onstage."

She waited for more. There had to be more. "That doesn't make any sense," she said. "He committed suicide because she made him come out at night? That's the big secret? That's ridiculous.

That's the most ridiculous thing I've ever heard."

"Tradition has always been important to the Coffeys," Vance said. "And Logan was a very sensitive, very troubled young man. His suicide almost drove the Coffeys away. If they'd left and taken their money with them, Mullaby would have been ruined. That was the last straw. No one wanted anything to do with Dulcie after that, after what she had cost the Coffey family, after what she had almost cost the town. She finally did something no one would forgive her for, something I couldn't buy her way out of."

Emily was several feet away before she realized she was backing away from him.

"I haven't spoken of it in twenty years," Vance said. "And I was going to keep it from you, because you were better off not knowing. The Coffeys obviously thought differently. I'm sorry."

Emily continued to back away. Vance simply watched her go, as if leaving him was what he expected, what he was used to. Without another word, Emily turned and walked back into the house.

When she reached her room, she just stood there, not knowing what to do. Coming here had been a mistake. A huge mistake. She should have known her mother had a good reason for keeping this place from Emily. This place wasn't right. There was something distinctly off about it. She'd felt it all along. People here committed suicide just for breaking tradition. *For coming out at night.* And this person everyone remembered as Dulcie Shelby wasn't her mother at all.

As she stood there, she began to hear a slight fluttering sound, like something was in the room with her.

She quickly looked up and around, and couldn't believe what she saw. She turned in a full circle, staggering slightly.

The wallpaper didn't have lilacs on it anymore.

It had changed to tiny butterflies of every imaginable color.

Out of the corner of her eye, she could have sworn she saw a few of them fluttering. There wasn't a pattern, they were simply *everywhere.* There was a static frenzy to them, like they desperately wanted out. Out of this room. Out of this town.

She walked over to the wall by the bed and put her hand to the paper.

Setting aside her incredulity for a moment, she knew exactly what they felt like.

She lowered her hand and slowly backed out of the room, then she ran back down the stairs. Vance was just now making his way into the kitchen from the yard.

"The wallpaper in my room," she said breathlessly. "When did you change it?"

He smiled. "The first time is always the hardest. You'll get used to it."

"The wallpaper looks old. How did you get it to look like that? How did you get it up so fast? How do you get it to . . . move?"

"I didn't do it. It just happens." He waved his arms like a magician. "It started with my sister. No one knows why. It's the only room in the house that does that, so you can move to any other bedroom, if you want."

She shook her head. This was too much craziness for one day. "I'm not a child, Grandpa Vance. Wallpaper doesn't change on its own."

Instead of arguing, he asked, "What did it change to?"

As if he didn't know. "Butterflies. Crazy butterflies!"

"Just think of that room as a universal truth," Grandpa Vance said. "How we see the world changes all the time. It all depends on our mood."

She took a deep breath and tried to be tactful. "I appreciate that you want it to be something magical, and I'm sure it took a lot of effort, but I don't care for that pattern. Can I paint over it?"

"Won't work," he told her, shrugging. "Your mother tried. Paint doesn't stick to that wallpaper. Won't tear off, either."

She paused. No one in this town would give an inch. Not with her mother. Not with this . . . wallpaper situation. "So what you're saying is, I'm stuck with the mood room."

"Unless you want to move."

Emily leaned back against the red refrigerator, because standing on her own suddenly seemed too much of a task. Grandpa Vance watched her silently. She didn't realize until that moment that he listed to one side, as if his left hip hurt him. "I'm still waiting for someone to tell me this is all just a trick being played on me," she finally said.

"I know that feeling well," he said quietly.

She met his eyes. "Does it get better?"

"Eventually."

Not the answer she wanted. But she was going to have to live with it.

What choice did she have? She had nowhere else to go.

OVER SEVENTY years ago, during the full moon in February—people called it the Snow Moon—when Piney Woods Lake froze solid and the aquatic plants trapped in the ice looked like fossils as kids skated over them, the house beside the Coffey mansion on Main Street caught fire.

Flames were jetting out of the windows of the house by the time the fire engine arrived. The vehicle had to be pushed there by the six strongest men in town because it wouldn't start in the cold. The town gathered in the park across the street to watch, huddled together under blankets, clouds of ice from their breath hovering above them. Vance was only four years old at the time, and his height was not yet a concern to anyone in his family. In fact, at the time, his father had actually been proud of what a strapping boy he had. Vance was wearing a red hat that night. It had a ball on top that his older sister, who was standing close behind him as they shared a single blanket, kept batting playfully back and forth.

Everyone watching the fire was riveted by the undulating yellow-golds and blue-oranges. It was like watching a memory of summer that the dark, relentless winter had almost made them forget. Some were so mesmerized, so ready for warmer weather and an end to aching joints, frozen commodes, and skin so dry it cracked and fell away like paper, that they walked dangerously close to the burning house and had to be hauled back by firemen, covered in soot.

First one person saw it, and then another, and soon the entire crowd was watching, not the fire, but the house next door—the Coffey mansion. All the servants were leaning out the windows on the side of the house facing the fire, and they were throwing whatever liquid substance they had on hand at the flames next door, trying to keep the fire away from the Coffey mansion. They threw water from flower vases, jars of peaches swimming in juice, a snow globe from one of the children's rooms, a leftover cup of tea from breakfast.

The town watched in awe, and slowly began to realize that the Coffeys weren't coming out and their loyal house staff was bravely trying to save them.

The fire was eventually extinguished and the Coffey mansion wasn't affected, except for some burnt azalea bushes that the cold had killed anyway. The next morning, the story began to circulate that the Coffeys had huddled in their basement while the fire had raged next door, claiming they would rather die than come out at night.

People had always known about the Coffeys' aversion to the dark hours, but no one had ever realized just how serious they were about it. It was the first time the citizens of Mullaby began to wonder, What if it wasn't that they *didn't* come out at night . . .

What if it was because they *couldn't*.

Dulcie had loved that story when she was a little girl. Sometimes Vance had to tell her twice before she would go to bed. Dulcie had always been close to her mother, but she'd never wanted much to do with him. Maybe because he'd been so cautious around her when she was a baby. She'd been so unbelievably small compared to him. He'd been scared of accidentally stepping on her, or losing her in his broad hands when he picked her up. So when he'd found something, like stories of the Coffeys, that brought Dulcie closer to him, he'd been thrilled. He hadn't known at the time that he'd been building the framework for disaster. By the time she was a teenager, she'd been obsessed with the Coffeys.

He didn't want that for Emily.

After Emily had gone to bed that night, Vance moved a chair to the back porch and waited, a flashlight in one hand, a piece of clover for courage in his other. The full July Buck Moon was out—a time for the young and randy.

The Mullaby lights had been around a long time, and there were dozens of stories about them. But after the fire, the rumor started that the Mullaby lights were really the ghosts of Coffey family members who had passed on, running free at night in death as they were never able to in life. That rumor stuck, and to this day, it was still what the people of Mullaby told all outsiders who asked.

When the light appeared in the woods that night, he stood and turned on his flashlight.

"Go back to where you came from," he called softly, knowing it could hear him. "I know what my daughter did to you. But you can't have Emily."

Chapter 9

*L*ate Monday afternoon, Julia was walking home from the post office, a bundle of mail in her arms. She was reeling from the news she'd just received.

As she turned the corner to Shelby Road, she lifted the postcard from the top of the bundle again.

She still couldn't believe it.

The postcard was from Nancy, one of her best friends in Baltimore. Because Julia couldn't afford a phone in her apartment while living here, once a month or so Nancy would write with what was going on with Julia's old group of friends—a rowdy group of young professionals who drank cocktails and talked a lot without saying very much. Julia had suspected that they'd been popular kids in high school, and she liked that they thought she was one of them. This particular postcard had thrown Julia for loop. On it, Nancy—whom Julia didn't even know was seeing anyone—had written that she had suddenly gotten married. She'd also written that their friend Devon had moved to Maine and their friend Thomas was taking a job in Chicago. Nancy promised to give Julia all the details as soon as she got home from her honeymoon in Greece.

Her honeymoon.

In Greece.

Julia hadn't expected everything to remain static while she was away, she just didn't think things would change *so much*. And all at once. She thought there would be more to come back to. But now, when she left Mullaby and moved back to Baltimore, there would be hardly any friends to reconnect with. That had been part of the plan, part of what had been keeping her going.

She tried to rally. She still had her Blue-Eyed Girl Bakery dream. The bakery, after all, was the whole reason she was doing this, the reason she had confined herself to this hell for two years. Growing apart from her friends had always been a risk. Blank-slate friendships were thin and temperamental. She knew that. There was no history there to cement people together, for better or worse.

So she would just deal with this.

She'd dealt with losing much worse.

She heard a splashing sound, and looked down the sidewalk to see Emily in front of Vance's house. There was a sudsy bucket by her feet, a sponge in her hand, and a large old car at the curb, a car that was steadfastly refusing to get clean despite Emily's effort. And it was a lot of effort. Work-off-your-frustration effort.

Julia tucked the postcard into one of the catalogs in her bundle of mail, then walked over to Emily. She hadn't seen her since Saturday and wondered if she and her grandfather were communicating any better, if Vance had finally told her everything. She stopped a few feet away from her. "Nice car."

Emily looked up. Her fine blond hair, as usual, seemed suspended in midair, half up in a ponytail, half hanging down around her face. "Grandpa Vance is letting me drive it. His mechanic is picking it up tomorrow morning, but I pushed it out of the garage so I could wash it first."

"I didn't know Vance still had this." Julia walked over to the car and leaned down to look in a dusty window. "It belonged to his wife, didn't it?"

"Yes."

Julia watched Emily scrub the hood for a few moments. "Have you talked to your grandfather?"

"Yes." That one word conveyed all Julia needed to know. Emily used her forearm to push some hair out of her face, then resumed scrubbing. "I didn't know it was going to be like this. But my mom knew. I'm sure that's why she never came back, and why she never told me about this place. I'm beginning to think she wouldn't want me here."

Julia looked from Emily, to the car, and back again. If Julia had had a car at Emily's age, she knew exactly what she would have done. Hell, she was even thinking about it now. "Planning to leave?"

Emily looked surprised that Julia had caught on so quickly. She shrugged. "I don't have anywhere to go."

"Well, if you'll hold off for a little while, the Mullaby Barbecue Festival is this weekend. It's a pretty big deal around here. Do you want to go with me?"

Emily didn't look at her. "You don't have to do this, Julia."

"Do what?"

"Try so hard to be friends with me. My mom was cruel to you. You don't have to be nice to me."

Oh, hell. "So Vance told you that, too?"

"He said my mom used to tease you. What did she do?" Emily finally met her eyes. If she were any more sincere, she would dissolve into fresh air and blow away.

Julia shook her head. "You shouldn't worry about it. It has nothing to do with you."

"Please tell me."

"It's not exactly my shining moment, Em," Julia said. "But, if you must know, aside from the pink hair, black clothes, and black lipstick, I used to wear a studded leather choker that looked like a dog collar to school every day. Your mother would bring dog treats to school and throw them at me in the hallways. Once, she even gave me flea powder. When she didn't have anything on hand, she simply barked at me." She paused at the memory. She hadn't thought about that in a long time. "To be fair, I gave her a lot to make fun of. You've seen the photos. I probably brought it on myself."

"Don't. Don't justify it. No one should ever compromise the dignity of another human being." She shook her head. "My mom taught me that. Can you believe it?"

"Yes, actually," Julia said. "I can."

"You told me she was popular."

"She was popular."

"But no one liked her?"

Julia thought about it for a moment. "Logan Coffey did."

Emily dropped the sponge she was holding into the bucket at her feet. "I'm sorry for what she did to you."

"I would never blame you for something your mother did, sweetheart. No one worth your time would. You're not who your mother was. In fact, I'm beginning to think you are who your mother *became*. It might be worth staying, if just to prove that to everyone."

Emily seemed to be thinking it over when they both heard a car door slam. They turned to see Sawyer standing beside a white Lexus hybrid parked behind Julia's truck next door.

He took off his sunglasses and tucked them into the collar of his shirt, then walked toward them.

"Is he here for your date?" Emily asked.

Julia turned to her. "What date?"

"He asked you out for Monday night. When we were at the lake."

Julia threw her head back and groaned. "Oh, damn."

Emily laughed. "You forgot? You forgot you had a date with *him*?"

"Sort of." Julia looked at her and smiled, glad that at least Emily was finding some humor in this.

"Hello, ladies," Sawyer said from behind her.

"Hi, Sawyer. Julia didn't forget you were going out," Emily said. "She's . . . just running late. It's my fault. She was going to change when I stopped her to show her my car. Right, Julia?"

Julia looked at her strangely before realizing that Emily thought she was *helping*. "Right," Julia said. "Let me know about going to the festival on Saturday, okay?"

"I will."

Julia turned and took Sawyer's arm and led him next door. "She thinks you're here to take me on a date," she leaned into him and whispered. "And she just went to a lot of trouble to help me save face because she thought I forgot. Go along with it, okay?"

"Okay," he said amiably as they walked up the steps to Stella's house. "But I *am* here to take you out. And obviously you *did* forget."

They entered the house and Julia set her mail on the table in the foyer. "I'm not going on a date with you," she said.

"You accepted in front of Emily. And she just covered for you. What kind of example are you setting?"

"That's a low blow. Just wait here until she goes inside."

He went to the living room window and pushed the curtain aside. "That might take a while. That car is filthy."

Julia smiled. "She seems thrilled with it."

"How was she when you took her home Saturday? She seems okay now."

"She's coping. Her grandfather finally told her some things about her mother's time here. I think she'll be better prepared for snubs from the Coffeys now."

"She really is nothing like Dulcie." He let the curtain fall, then walked over to Stella's striped silk couch—the one she didn't let people sit on—and sat, crossing his legs and stretching his arms over the back. She found herself staring at him. He was just so perfect. "You do realize that the longer I stay in here, the more likely she is to think we're doing something scandalous," he said.

"Like what? Stealing Stella's furniture?"

"You're being obtuse."

"And you're being manipulative."

He shrugged. "If that's what it takes, then I have no problem with it."

"Careful, Sawyer, you're acting a lot like you did when you were sixteen. And here I was thinking you'd improved so much."

"And there it is," he said with satisfaction.

"What?"

"Exactly what I want to talk about."

She'd walked right into that. "No," she said. "Stella will be home any minute."

"She won't be home for an hour or more." He locked eyes with her, holding her there on the spot. "You said you've forgiven me. Is that true?"

"I'm not doing this. I'm not having this conversation." She shook her head adamantly.

"Why?"

"Because it's mine, Sawyer!" she said. "It's *my* memory and *my* regret. It's not yours. I'm not

143

sharing it with you. You didn't want it then. You can't have it now."

The words were strung in the air like garland. She could almost see them.

Sawyer stood and she thought for a moment that he was walking toward her, and she hastily took a few steps back. But she soon discovered that he was walking to the fireplace mantel in Stella's living room. He stopped there and put his hands in his pockets, staring into the empty fireplace. "Holly and I couldn't have kids."

Julia paused at this sudden change in subject. Sawyer and Holly had gotten married right out of college. Her father had told Julia about it in passing one year. It had hurt a little, but hadn't surprised her much. Sawyer and Holly had dated since middle school. What had surprised her, when she moved back to Mullaby, was discovering that their marriage had lasted less than five years. Everyone, including her, thought they'd be together forever. Julia in particular knew all that Sawyer had done to preserve his relationship with Holly when they were teens.

"The ironic thing is, *I* was the problem," Sawyer continued. "I contracted chicken pox my senior year in college and had an unusual reaction to it. There's not a week that goes by that I don't think of what happened between us, Julia, and how I responded. My fear and my stupidity not only made what was already a horrible time in your life worse, it destroyed what turned out to be my only chance to father a child. *That's* what I wanted to tell you. I knew the moment I saw you again that you were holding on to what had happened, that I was still, in your eyes, that stupid, stupid boy. Maybe this will make you feel a little better."

"Feel better?" she asked incredulously.

He shrugged. "To know that I got what I had coming."

For the first time, Julia realized Sawyer might be just as messed up as she was about what had happened. He was simply better at hiding it. "What is the matter with you?" she demanded. "How could you possibly think that would make me feel better?"

"It doesn't?"

"Of course not."

Still staring into the fireplace, he said, "I've read that an abortion rarely affects a woman's ability to bear more children. Is that true?"

She hesitated. "I assume so."

"I'm glad," he said softly.

This had been hers, and only hers, for so long. She didn't think he cared, or even deserved, to know what she'd been keeping so close to her heart, this hope she'd been carrying around for so long. "You bastard. I was happy being mad at you. Why couldn't you have just left it at that?"

He smiled slightly. "Because I get such a kick out of telling beautiful women that I'm sterile."

At that moment, the front door opened and there was Stella. She always smelled like carnations from her florist shop when she came in from work. The scent ran ahead of her into the room, like an excited pet.

"I told you she'd be home any minute," Julia said.

"Am I interrupting something?" Stella asked hopefully, looking back and forth from Julia to Sawyer. "I can come back later. As a matter of fact, I don't have to come back at all. I can be gone all night."

"You're not interrupting anything. Good night." Julia turned and jogged up the stairs to her apartment.

"Night?" Stella said. "It's barely five o'clock."

Julia locked the door behind her and went straight to her bedroom. She sat on the edge of the bed, then she fell back and stared at the long yellow squares of daylight stretching across the ceiling.

She suddenly had a very big decision to make, one she thought she'd never *have* to make.

Coming back here had messed up everything.

HER FIRST six weeks at Collier Reformatory in Maryland were hard. There were some tough girls there. Julia spent a lot of time crying in her bed in the dorm, and using all her allotted phone time trying to call Sawyer. His maid always said he wasn't home. Julia refused to call her father, or talk to him when he called, for doing this to her. Her therapist didn't pressure her. Her therapy sessions were odd at first, but then she started looking forward to them.

In fact, her therapist was the second person she told when realized she was pregnant.

Julia was thrilled when she found out. In her mind, it meant she could go home and be with Sawyer. They would get married and move in together and raise their child. He could make her happy. He could make her better. She knew he could. He *saw* her. He was the only person who did.

She called his house incessantly until she obviously wore the maid down. When Sawyer got on the phone, she was taken aback by his tone.

"Julia, you have to stop calling here," he said brusquely.

"I . . . I've missed you. Where have you been?"

Silence.

"This place is horrible," she went on. "They want to put me on medication."

Sawyer cleared his throat. "Maybe that's a good idea, Julia."

"No, it's not." She smiled, thinking how wonderful this was going to be. "It might hurt the baby."

Silence again. Then, "What baby?"

"I'm pregnant, Sawyer. I'm going to tell my therapist, and then my dad. I should be home soon."

"Wait, wait, wait," he said quickly. *"What?"*

"I know it's a surprise. It was for me, too. But, don't you see? It's really the best thing that could have happened. I'll come home and we can be together."

"Is it mine?" he asked.

She felt the first string tighten around her heart, thin and sharp. "Of course it's yours. That was my first time. You were my first."

He waited so long to say something that she thought he'd hung up. "Julia, I don't want a baby," he finally said.

"Well, it's too late for that," she said, trying to laugh.

"Is it?"

"What do you mean?"

"I'm sixteen!" He suddenly exploded. "I can't be a parent! And I'm with Holly. This is the *worst* thing that could happen to me right now! I have *plans*."

A second string, then a third, tightened around her insides, making it hard to breathe. "You're with Holly?" She knew he'd been dating Holly, but she'd assumed, after what had happened on the football field . . . the way he'd looked at her and touched her . . .

How could he do that to her and still be with Holly?

"I've always been with her. You know that. We're going to get married after college."

"But that night—"

He interrupted her, saying, "You were upset."

"It's not just the baby, then?" she almost whispered. "You don't want *me*?"

"I'm sorry. I really am. I thought you knew."

You thought I knew? Her eyes started filling with tears and her breathing was heavy. She thought she might hyperventilate.

He was supposed to save her.

"I'll take care of it," she said, turning to hang up the pay phone. Sawyer might not want the baby, but she did. She would take care of it by herself.

Sawyer misunderstood. "That's good. It's the right thing, Julia. I know it'll be hard, but it will be over before you know it. Just get an abortion and everything will be fine. Let me send you some money." His voice was so nice now, so relieved. She felt a wave of hatred so strong that it popped off her skin and caused a crinkling noise in the phone receiver.

An abortion? He wanted her to get an abortion? He didn't want the baby, but he didn't want her to have it either. How could she ever have thought she was in love with such a person? "No. I can do it by myself."

"Let me do something."

"You've done enough," she said, and hung up.

Telling her father was horrible. When her therapist made her call him, he wanted her to come home right away, thinking she'd gotten pregnant at

149

Collier. But she admitted that it had happened before she left Mullaby. Though he demanded to know who the father was, she never told him. In the end, everyone agreed that she should stay at Collier. She wasn't the only pregnant girl there, after all.

She started craving cakes around her third month. The sensation was unbelievable. There were times she thought she would go crazy with it. Her therapist told her it was just a normal pregnancy craving, but Julia knew better. This child growing inside her obviously had Sawyer's magical sweet sense. When Julia couldn't get enough sweets during the day, she started sneaking out of her dorm to go to the cafeteria. That's where she baked her first cake. She became pretty good at it after a while, because it was the only thing that settled the baby. It had an unusual effect on the rest of the school, too. The smell of cake would slowly waft through the hallways while she baked at night, and girls in their dorm rooms, even the girls whose dreams were always dark, would suddenly dream of their kindhearted grandmothers and long-ago birthday parties.

Julia's therapist started talking to her about adoption options in her fifth month. She adamantly refused to consider it. But every session her therapist would ask, *How do you plan to care for this child on your own?* And Julia began to get scared. She didn't know how she was going to do it. Her only choice was her father, but when she brought it up, he immediately said no. Beverly didn't want a baby in the house.

In the spring, in a flood of pain and fear so great she doubled over in French class, Julia went into labor. It came on so quickly that she actually gave birth in the ambulance on the way to the hospital. She could feel the baby's frustration, her impatience, as she maneuvered her way to freedom. And Julia couldn't stop her. As much as she wanted to, there was nothing she could do to keep this child physically bound to her any longer. Her daughter had a mind, and an agenda, all her own. After it was over, the baby proceeded to fuss about how hard her journey had been to anyone who would listen, the way old ladies in tweed coats liked to fuss about long, hot train rides into the city. It made Julia laugh, holding the squawking infant in her arms in the ambulance. She was perfect, with Sawyer's blond hair and blue eyes.

Julia's father came to Maryland to see her in the hospital the next day, and she asked him one last time to take her and the baby home.

Standing at the foot of the hospital bed, his ball cap in his hands, looking shy and out of place, he again said no. She gave up on ever having a real relationship with her father after that. Nothing would ever be the same.

It was the hardest decision Julia had ever made, giving up her little girl. Now that the baby was independent of Julia's body, she knew she couldn't take care of her alone. She could barely take care of herself. She hated Beverly for not wanting a baby in the house, and she hated her father for being so weak. But most of all, she hated Sawyer. If only he had loved her. If only he had been there to help her. Then she could have kept the baby. He was depriving her of the one person in the world who would ever need her completely, the only person in the world she knew she would love for the rest of her life. No questions. No limits.

She was told that a couple from Washington, D.C., adopted the baby. Julia was given two photos. One was the official hospital photo, the other was of Julia in the hospital bed holding her —warm and soft and smelling pink. Julia put the photos away immediately, because it hurt too much to look at them, only to find them years later in an old textbook when she was packing to move after college.

It took a long, long time to feel fine again. She started cutting herself again not long after she was released from the hospital. Her school therapist worked tirelessly to get her admitted into a summer program sponsored by Collier because Julia wasn't ready to go home. Julia still felt too vulnerable to go back to Mullaby after the summer, so her father agreed that she should stay at Collier for her senior high school year.

She applied to and was accepted to college the

next year. Though she hadn't baked since she was pregnant, those months of practice made her proficient enough to get a job at a grocery store bakery to help her father pay for her college tuition. By this time, with the help of continued therapy sessions, Julia was able to think of Sawyer without the world turning a furious ember red around her, and she remembered what he'd told her about following the scent of his mother's cakes home. It became a symbol to her. Maybe one day in the future, baking cakes would bring her daughter—who had a sweet sense like her father—back to Julia. Then she would explain why she gave her up. At the very least, it would carry Julia's love to her.

Wherever she was.

Nearly twenty years later, Julia was still calling out to her. Knowing she was out there in the world somewhere was what got Julia through every single day. She couldn't imagine a life without knowing that.

Sawyer was living that unimaginable life.

It was then that she knew she had to tell him.

She thought she'd been miserable here before.

The next six months were going to be hell.

JULIA HEARD a light tapping at her door. She opened her eyes and was surprised to see that the sky was blackberry blue and the first star of the night was out. She got up and went to her bedroom doorway.

153

"Julia?" Stella called. "Julia, are you all right? You've been awfully quiet up here. Sawyer's gone, if that's what you're waiting for." There was a pause. "Okay. I'll be downstairs if you need me. If you want to talk."

She heard Stella walk back down the stairs.

Julia rested her head against the doorjamb for a moment, then she walked into the hallway. She paused at the door to the stairs, then walked past it and into the kitchen.

A hummingbird cake, she decided as she turned on the kitchen light. It was made with bananas and pineapples and pecans and had a cream cheese frosting.

She would make it light enough to float away.

She reached over to open the window.

To float to her daughter.

Chapter 10

*T*he car had an eight-track player.

The steering wheel was huge, like it should be on a boat.

The interior smelled like cough drops.

And she loved it.

Emily loved this car.

When Vance's mechanic dropped the car off that next day, she eagerly sat behind the wheel. But then she realized that she couldn't think of anywhere she wanted to go. The more she thought about it, the more she didn't really want to leave Mullaby. Although she would never say it out loud—she would never tell another living soul—there was a part of her now finding an odd comfort in her mother's fallibility. Dulcie had set an impossible standard in Boston, and Emily thought she could never do enough, care enough, work hard enough. And sometimes she'd resented it, which made her feel even worse. But it turns out even Dulcie herself couldn't live up to that standard. At least not here.

Emily sat in the car until it became too hot, then she got out. She couldn't go next door to visit, because Julia had left earlier. And she didn't want to go back inside her own house, because Grandpa Vance was taking a nap, and the new butterfly wallpaper in her room made her nervous. She would *swear* it moved sometimes, and she couldn't figure out how. She walked aimlessly to the back of the house. The yard was so overgrown that, at eye level, it was hard to even see the gazebo at the back of the property. Looking around, she was amazed that she'd come away with only a cut on her heel that night she'd chased the Mullaby lights.

She hadn't seen the light in the woods since she'd come back from the lake, and she was a little disappointed. Making sense of at least one thing here would be nice.

With nothing better to do, she began to pick up

155

twigs and fallen limbs from the yard. She checked the garage for a lawn mower, but didn't find one. She did find some shears, though, and went to the gazebo and began to trim back the wild boxwood bushes, flustering a large frog who was hiding in the shade there.

As she slowly worked her way around the gazebo, shortening the bushes so the posts and latticework could be seen, the fat frog followed her.

At one point, she lobbed off a bit of boxwood and a twig fell onto the frog. She laughed and bent to lift it off of him, and that's when she saw it.

A large heart with the initials D.S. + L.C. carved inside.

It was carved onto a back post of the gazebo, near the bottom, just like on the tree at the lake.

Her fingers reached out to trace the lines of the heart. Logan Coffey had been in this backyard. She didn't know why her eyes went to the woods, just a hunch, but there, on one of the trees that formed the border into the woods, was another carving.

D.S. + L.C.

She set the shears down on the steps of the gazebo and went to it. The frog followed her for a few steps, then stopped. She saw another heart farther in the woods. Then another. They formed a trail, too irresistible not to follow. Every three or four trees, there was a heart with the initials inside. Some of them were harder to find than others, and she spent at least fifteen minutes slowly making her way through the woods, until she finally broke into a clearing.

This was exactly the same place the light had led her the night she'd chased it.

The park on Main Street.

She looked over to the bandstand, and there, carved into the base of the structure, next to the side steps, was the heart with the initials.

She walked to the bandstand and knelt, touching the carving.

Why did they lead here? Did they have something to do with her mother leading Logan Coffey onto the bandstand stage that night?

She stood again and looked around the park. It was full of people that day. Some were having lunch, some were sunbathing. A couple of people were playing Frisbee with their dogs.

And then there was Win Coffey.

He was standing with a few adults in the middle of the park. One of the men was the big man from the party at the lake. She didn't realize it before, but he was clearly related to Win—if the dark hair, the summer linen suit, and the bow tie were any indication. The adults were gesturing toward the street, to the large festival banner being erected, but Win's head was turned the other way, looking at her.

Without thinking, she ducked behind the bandstand. Then she immediately regretted it. What was the matter with her? In a small town, it was inevitable that they would run into each other. But she didn't want him to think she was following him. Not that hiding as soon as she saw him helped that impression.

She waited a few minutes before she straightened her shoulders and walked back around the bandstand. It was a public park. She had as much of a right to be here as he did.

As soon as she came around from the back, she gave an exclamation of surprise.

There he was, facing her. He was leaning one shoulder against the side of the bandstand, his hands in his trouser pockets.

"Are you hiding from me?" he asked.

"No," she said quickly. "I mean, I didn't know you'd be here. I didn't even know *I'd* be here. I was just following a trail of these from the back of my grandfather's house." She pointed to the carving.

Without moving, he lowered his eyes to the heart. "They're all over town. After my uncle died, my grandfather tried to scratch over all of them, until he realized there were too many around, more than he'd probably ever find."

"Dulcie Shelby and Logan Coffey. That's what they mean?"

He nodded.

"Despite what everyone thinks of her, she wasn't this person," she found herself saying as she indicated the carving again. "Not when she left."

"I know," he said. When she raised her brows, he shrugged. "I Googled her name the day after we met. I found out a lot about her. I read about the school she helped found in Boston. And I saw your photo on the school's website."

That made her cheeks feel like she'd bitten into a green apple. She hoped it wasn't the photo of her at the Christmas food drive. She looked constipated in that photo, yet it was always the one they used in the school literature. When Emily had protested, her mother had said, *Don't be vain. What you look like doesn't matter. It's the deed that matters.* Emily used to think her mother had no idea what it was like to be a teenager. "You know a lot more about me than I know about you," Emily finally said. "I don't think that's fair."

Win leaned in toward her, making her heart do a strange kick. His eyes went to her lips, and she suddenly wondered if he was going to kiss her. The crazy thing was, despite everything, there was a tiny part of her that wanted him to. "Does this mean you're curious?" he asked.

"Yes," she said honestly, swallowing. "Especially about why coming out at night caused your uncle to commit suicide. My mother might not have been a very nice person here, but what kind of secret is that to kill yourself over?"

She didn't realize what she'd said until he suddenly pulled back and gave her an assessing look. "You've learned a few things since we last talked."

"My grandfather said he didn't tell me because he thought I was better off not knowing. He's not thrilled that you took it upon yourself to be my tour guide into my mother's past."

"And how do *you* feel?"

"I still love my mom."

He hesitated, as if this was a side effect of his actions he hadn't intended. "I wasn't trying to make you feel otherwise. I'm sorry. I was just trying to help."

Something made her wonder if he meant help her, or help himself. "Why was it such a big deal to be seen at night?" she suddenly asked. "I mean, you come out at night now, don't you?"

"No."

"No?" she asked, surprised. "Why?"

"You wouldn't believe me if I told you."

"You've said that before. How do you know?"

He gave her a look that made every nerve in her body feel alive. Like when someone comes up behind you and startles you—there's a small, sudden twitch, a quick gasp of air. "Be careful what you wish for," he said.

"Win, what are you doing back here?" The man dressed like Win suddenly appeared from around the front of the bandstand. He was bulky but not fat, as if his own importance made him take up so much room. He smelled of cigars and sweet laundry starch. He looked at Win, who tightened like a rope knot with clear animosity. The man's eyes then fell on Emily. "Ah," he said, as if some-thing suddenly made sense. "You must be Emily Benedict."

"Yes."

He gave her a politician's smile, lots of teeth, but it didn't quite make it to his eyes. "I'm Morgan Coffey, mayor of Mullaby. And Win's father. I believe I saw you at my daughter's party last Saturday? I don't recall you being invited."

"I didn't know I needed an invitation. I apolo-gize."

"Well then." He held out his hand and she shook it. His grip was bone-crushing. "Welcome to town."

"Thank you," she said, trying to draw her hand back.

But he held on, lifting her arm slightly, his eyes on the silver charm bracelet she was wearing. "Where did you get this?" he demanded.

With another tug, she slid her hand out of his and hid the bracelet with her other hand. "It was my mother's."

Morgan Coffey looked completely poleaxed. "My father gave that to my mother when they got married."

Emily shook her head. Surely he was mistaken. "Maybe they just look the same."

"The moon charm has an inscription: *Yours from dark to light.*"

Emily didn't have to look. The words had almost

been rubbed off, but they were still there. She could feel tears come to her eyes. "I'm sorry," she said, fumbling as she took it off. She held the bracelet out to him, her heart breaking. "She must have stolen it." After what she'd learned about her mother, she wouldn't put it past her.

A muscle twitched at his jawline. "She didn't steal it. Win, let's go." Morgan Coffey turned and left without another word.

Without taking the bracelet.

Win watched him go, then said to Emily, "That went better than I thought it would, actually."

She looked away, blinking back the tears. "I don't think I want to know how you thought it would go."

He smiled and stepped over to her. He took the bracelet, which she was still holding out in her palm, and put it back on her wrist.

His touch was warm, and it seemed greater than him, somehow, like she could feel it beyond the places he actually touched. And there again was that comforting feeling. She took a deep breath, her tears disappearing. How did he do that, make her feel so wary, and yet so *fond* of him?

He looked up from fastening the bracelet and met her eyes. He was still touching her wrist, and she was trembling with the effort to remain still. "Will I see you at the festival this weekend?"

Julia had asked her, but Emily hadn't given her an answer yet. But she had the answer now. "Yes."

"Friends?" he asked, and it sounded like he was asking her to do something perilous. He made her feel *brave* for standing there, for facing him, and she didn't know why. She'd never felt brave before. Not like this, like there were choices she could finally make on her own.

She nodded. "Friends."

WHEN SAWYER pulled into his driveway after work that day, he saw Julia sitting on the front steps of his townhouse, a white cake box on her lap. It never occurred to him that she knew where he lived. It made him feel important to her, somehow. Though that was probably his delusion speaking. It spoke to him often about Julia. But this explained the black pickup truck he saw parked at the curb a couple of blocks away. As he'd passed it, he'd thought it looked like Julia's, though he had no idea why she chose to park so far away. He wondered if she didn't want to be seen associating with him.

He stopped in front of his garage and cut the engine. He stepped out of his Lexus, bringing his briefcase with him. He'd been looking at potential rental properties that day. His family's property management business was slowly expanding into neighboring counties. His father had been against it at first. For a very long time, their only client had been the Coffeys, who owned most of the rental property in Mullaby. It had been a constant battle with his father to get him to even entertain the idea of taking on other properties to manage. Now business was so good they were considering opening a satellite office.

As he approached her, Julia stood. She was wearing blue jeans and a dark blue peasant blouse, the ties of the neck open. She looked so beautiful and soft, with her big brown eyes and her light brown hair shining in the afternoon light. He couldn't see the pink streak, and he had an incredible urge to find it. He'd always been fascinated by her, drawn to her the way curious people are always drawn to things they don't understand. But he'd done a spectacular job of ruining any chance he'd ever had of being with her, and he'd done it at the amazing age of sixteen. Truly, he should get an award or something. World's Longest Regret.

The night he and Julia had had was amazing, and something he'd dreamed about for years. Up until that night, she'd only been a fantasy. He'd been the popular preppy kid; she'd been the school's punk hardass. He'd never thought he'd have a chance with her, so he'd kept his distance and watched her from afar. That night was everything he'd dreamed it would be, although a little bittersweet. He'd meant—absolutely—everything he'd said at the time, all caught up in the fantasy come true. But adolescence is like having only enough light to see the step directly in front of you, and no farther. When Julia had left for school the next day, he'd gotten scared. He and Holly had the approval of not only his parents and hers, but everyone in school. Especially after what had happened with Dulcie and Logan that same summer, how the whole town had turned on her and looked suspiciously at her friends, he'd wanted to hold on to what he had, and he didn't have Julia. Julia was water in his hands. She'd slipped right through. Lovely and strange and unpredictable, she'd been everything he wasn't. Nothing he was used to. He'd reacted badly when she'd called him and told him she was pregnant. When he thought back to that conversation, it was like watching a movie. It was the only way he could deal with it, to totally disassociate. That wasn't him. That was a ghost of himself, some horrible boy who'd forced a troubled girl to have an abortion because he hadn't wanted to face the consequences of his actions.

But he ended up facing the consequences anyway. Fate has a way of biting you in the ass like that. He thought he'd moved on, first with Holly, then by throwing himself into the family business. But then Julia came back to town and he realized for the first time that he hadn't moved on at all.

He'd just been waiting.

Waiting for her to come back and forgive him.

"I didn't know you knew where I lived," he said as he walked up the steps toward her.

"Apparently, I didn't. Someone told me once that you owned that big house on Gatliff Street. I assumed you lived there. But Stella told me that's where you and Holly lived when you were together, and that you'd moved here after the divorce."

"Holly and I still own that house jointly, actually." He stopped on the porch and stood in front of her. "When she moved to Raleigh, we agreed to rent it out and split the income."

"Why didn't you just keep living there?"

"It was too big. My family gave it to us as a wedding gift. Five bedrooms. It was a big hint for grandchildren."

"Oh," Julia said awkwardly.

"Don't be embarrassed. I'm not. I've come to terms with it."

She gave him a look that said she didn't believe him. Then, changing the subject, she thrust the cake box at him. "I brought you a hummingbird cake," she said. "I made it last night."

He set down his briefcase and took the box from her, stunned. "You actually baked me a cake?"

"Don't get all emotional on me. I have to tell you something. A couple of things, actually. I'll save the big thing for later."

Later. That was curious. And encouraging. He couldn't help it. Later meant there would be time in between. Time to be with her. "And the cake is to soften me up?"

"The cake is because I know you like it."

He gestured toward the door. "Come in," he said, suddenly excited by the thought of her being in his house. It was almost as if, by having her step over the threshold, something significant would be accomplished. She would be closer to him. He would be closer to her forgiveness.

But she shook her head. "I can't. I ran out of gas coming over here."

"Ah. That's why I saw your truck parked a couple of blocks away."

She nodded. "I was just waiting for you to come home to give you this and to tell you something, then I have to walk to the gas station."

"I can take you."

"I'll be fine," she said dismissively. She didn't want anything from him. Yet he wanted so much from her. "I do bake cakes because of you. Well, I *started* baking cakes because of you. That's what I wanted to tell you."

He wasn't expecting that. He rocked back slightly on his heels.

She stuffed her hands deep into her jeans pockets, making her shoulders hunch a little. "It was what you told me about how you always sensed when your mother baked cakes. I loved that story. I started baking when I was away at school. That's a whole story unto itself. The point is, at a time in my life when there were a lot of bad things happening, you gave me something good. Something to hold on to. I'm opening my own bakery when I move back to Baltimore. And it all started with you."

He felt incredibly humbled. She was being too generous. "I didn't give you anything but a hard time. How can you possibly appreciate that?"

"I've learned to hold on to the good parts."

He didn't know what to say. He struggled for a few moments before saying, "And that's not even the big thing?"

She smiled. "No."

On the one hand, he really wanted to know. On the other, he wanted to make this last. As curious as he was, he would live with the anticipation forever if it meant being able to be with her like this.

He shifted the cake box and opened it. He loved hummingbird cake. It was all he could do not to dig his hand through it like a shovel right now. His mother had tried to hide cakes from him when he was small, but he always found them. He couldn't help it. At that age, he hadn't yet developed the willpower to resist. He'd inherited his sweet sense from his grandfather. It was the reason he felt so close to him, closer than to anyone else in his family. His grandfather had been the one who taught him how to turn it off, after one too many stomachaches. And he'd also been the one who'd told Sawyer that not everyone could see what he saw, so be careful who he told. Sawyer normally left it off now, unless he was distracted or tired, then he would unwittingly see the silver glitter undulating out of house windows, or the sparkle trailing out of a child's lunch box. The only time he consciously switched it on was when Julia baked on Thursday nights. She was hidden from him, but he could see her do this. She was so good at it, the smell so beautiful. And he'd inspired it. He was overwhelmed.

"You're the only person I've ever told about my sweet sense," he said. He'd never even told his ex-wife.

"I hate to break this to you, but your secret is out."

He closed the lid to the box before temptation got the better of him. He shook his head. "Uh-uh. That's not going to work anymore. You can be as hard and sarcastic as you want, but we both know you really have a soft spot for me. You just admitted it."

"If you tell anyone, I'll deny it."

"Come on," he said, feeling as light as high cotton. "I'll take you to your truck. I think I even have some gas in a canister in my garage."

"No, I . . ."

But he had already grabbed his briefcase and was walking down the steps.

By the time he had the cake and his briefcase in the backseat of the car and the gas canister full of gas in the trunk, she was in the driveway, looking uncomfortable and ridiculously lovely.

He opened the passenger side door for her, and she sighed and got in.

When Sawyer got behind the wheel and started

the car, she busied herself by playing with his navigation system. He just smiled when she programmed his GPS to take them to Frank's Toilet World on the highway.

Instead of Toilet World, in a matter of minutes, he was at her truck. They both got out and he put the gas from the canister into her tank. She thanked him, but before she could get in, he said impulsively, "Have dinner with me tonight."

She shook her head. "That's not a good idea."

"Come on. You have six months left here. Live a little."

She snorted. "Are you seriously asking me to have a fling with you?"

"Absolutely not," he said, feigning shock. "I said dinner. It was your lascivious mind that went to the bedroom."

She smiled, and he was glad. This was much better than the bristle she'd given him since coming back. Without thinking, he lifted his hand to her hair, petting it, then threading his fingers through it so that he could see the pink streak. He'd often wondered why she kept it. It had to have something to do with her pink hair when she was a teenager. Was it her way of remembering? Or maybe it was her reminder to never go back.

When he met her eyes, he was stunned to see that they were huge. They darted once to his lips.

She thought he was going to kiss her.

And she wasn't running away.

Suddenly his blood was pumping thickly, increasing in a steady rhythm until it was roaring in his ears. And he leaned down and put his lips to hers.

Touching her, kissing her, was everything he remembered. There was such chemistry between them. Christ, he could almost feel it, the break in her exterior. She'd just let him in. It was that effortless. He remembered from the football field, how willingly she had given herself to him, how it had felt like this. And he remembered thinking at the time, *This girl must be in love with me.*

He lifted his lips from hers, startled.

"I have to go," she said quickly, not meeting his eyes, obviously embarrassed. "Thank you for the gas." She wrenched open the door to her truck and jumped in.

He was still standing on the sidewalk long after she drove away.

What just happened here? he thought.

What in the hell just happened?

Chapter 11

*L*ong ago and mostly forgotten, the land surrounding Mullaby was once farmland, hog land. In those hardscrabble days of North Carolina, when cattle refused to thrive, swine farming was a boon to the state. Like the citizens of many small towns in the area, the people of

Mullaby took great pride in the slow, meticulous pit-cooking of pork, and it soon became an important part of defining who they were. It was at first a Sunday tradition, then a symbol of community, and eventually an art form, the art of old North Carolina, an art born out of work so hard it could fell a hearty man.

But as the years passed, the small farms and the once-prosperous hog-trade trails that stretched into Tennessee gradually disappeared. Up cropped neighborhoods and shopping centers, and then the interstate came, taking away people who remembered and bringing in people who didn't. Eventually the origin and the reasons fell away from the bone, and all that was left was a collective unconscious, a tradition without a memory, a dream every person in the town of Mullaby had on the same date every year.

In the early hours of the morning on the day of the Mullaby Barbecue Festival, a fog would settle low in the air, sneaking into windows and into nighttime visions. *You'll forget when you wake,* it would whisper, *but know this now and be proud.*

This is your history.

STELLA HAD been gone for hours before Julia finally left the house. Stella considered the festival her day of debauchery. She started early and wouldn't be home until the next day. Sometimes Julia worried about her. She couldn't help it. She'd gotten to know Stella well in the past year and a half. Julia had never seen anyone *try so hard* to be happy with what she had.

The Stella that Julia knew now was very different from the Stella she'd known in high school. Back then, Stella had been conspicuously showy, just like Dulcie Shelby. They'd been as thick as thieves. She'd driven a shiny black BMW bought specifically to match her shiny black hair. And Julia remembered hearing about how Stella's decorator mother, who lived in Raleigh while Stella lived in Mullaby with her father, had designed Stella's bedroom to look like a movie theater, complete with her own private movie screen and a popcorn machine. It had even been featured in some design magazine. To be honest, when Julia came back, she'd been surprised to find Stella still living here. Julia had always imagined those rich girls from school going on to live exotic lives. They'd had everything, every opportunity. When you had that much, why would you squander it? How could you accept anything less?

Stella's problem, it turned out, was falling for the wrong guy. A tale as old as time. Her ex-husband had done a number on her by cheating and spending his way through her trust fund. The experience had turned Stella into a funny, self-deprecating woman who worked in a flower shop, lived in a house she could barely afford, and drank wine out of a box. Sometimes Julia wondered if

Stella wanted it all back, if she would trade all she'd learned to be that envied girl again.

Julia had never asked. Their pasts were touchy subjects, which was why Julia hadn't told her about Sawyer and the kiss, even though she really wanted to. And the fact that she couldn't bring herself to tell something that personal to Stella meant that they weren't as close as Stella thought they were. It made her sad, though she couldn't figure out why. Julia didn't want to get close to anyone here. Her real life was back in Baltimore.

It was noon when Julia finally walked over to Vance's house to take Emily to the Mullaby Barbecue Festival. She knocked on the door and heard Emily race down the staircase with uncharacteristic enthusiasm. Julia was instantly suspicious.

Emily ran outside, and Vance followed shortly.

"Are you sure you won't come with us?" Emily asked her grandfather, almost hopping from one foot to the other.

"I'm sure," Vance said. "You two have fun."

Julia and Vance watched as Emily ran down the front porch steps. "I'll have her back before dark," Julia told Vance. "And we'll bring you some festival treats."

"That's right nice of you, Julia. She seems awfully excited, doesn't she?" Vance said as Emily disappeared under the trees.

"Yes," Julia said thoughtfully. "She does."

174

"Getting excited about barbecue. She's a lot like me." He paused, then seemed to reconsider. "I mean, there's not a lot about me I'd want her to favor, but . . ."

Julia put her hand on his arm. "She *is* a lot like you, Vance. And that's a good thing."

When Julia met her on the sidewalk, Emily asked, "Why won't he come? He loves barbecue."

"Vance tries to stay away from crowds," Julia said as they walked toward downtown.

"I guess I've gotten so used to it that I forget sometimes."

"You're fitting in more than you think, then. So, how are the two of you getting along?"

Emily shrugged, distracted. "Okay, I guess. Better."

"That's good."

Once they reached Main Street, Julia could tell that Emily was a little taken aback. First-timers usually were. Most people assumed that because Mullaby was small, the festival would be small, as well. But the Mullaby Barbecue Festival was actually the largest barbecue festival in the Southeast, and it attracted people from all over the country. The street was closed to cars, and white tents stretched as far as the eye could see. In the distance, the top of a Ferris wheel could be seen. The smell was intense and delicious, like being in an oven.

As they wove their way through the crowded

175

street, they passed numerous barbecue tents, the focus of the festival, after all. Inside the tents, the barbecue sandwiches were made in an assembly line. Sauce, no sauce? Coleslaw on your sandwich? Want hush puppies in a cup with that? The sandwiches could be seen in the hands of every other person on the street, half-wrapped in foil. There were also tents selling pork rinds and boiled corn on the cob, chicken on a stick and brats, fried pickles and fried candy bars, and, of course, funnel cakes. Craft tents dotted the area, too.

"I didn't know it would be this big," Emily said, her head swinging around, trying to take it all in. "How do you find anyone in all of this?"

"Looking for someone in particular?" Julia asked.

Emily hesitated. "No. Not really."

But to test her theory, Julia purposely led Emily to the main stage. There were several stages staggered around the festival where bands were playing—folk and bluegrass mostly—but the main stage was right in the middle of Main Street. Crowds had to break around it like water.

There was a group of people, most of them Coffeys, clustered at the bottom of the stage steps, the men in hats and the women in crisp belted dresses. Win was wearing a straw boater hat, which would have looked ridiculous on anyone else his age. Sure enough, Emily's eyes went right to him. And he seemed to know exactly when it happened, because he looked up and saw her.

Neither of them moved toward the other, but their intense awareness was almost palpable.

"Why is Win . . . why are *the Coffeys* so dressed up?" Emily asked. "I mean, more than usual."

"Because this festival belongs to them. Their family created it as an annual event about sixty years ago. It's their baby. In a little while, they'll do all their grandstanding on that stage, then they'll judge some barbecue and pie contests."

Win's father looked over to his son, then followed his stare. He immediately called Win over to him, at the same time Julia ushered Emily away.

She and Emily had a good time for the next few hours. They ate way too much and bought commemorative T-shirts that read I WENT HOG WILD AT THE MULLABY BARBECUE FESTIVAL. It was a splurge Julia could hardly afford—she allotted herself very little spending money because she wanted as much as possible to go toward the restaurant's mortgage—but it was worth it.

Julia hadn't been to the festival in years. Her restaurant had a tent here, somewhere. She didn't have anything to do with it. Her managers had set it all up. She remembered how her father had loved the festival. And there had been a time when Julia had loved to come with him. She thought the event had lost its appeal for her, but she liked seeing it through Emily's eyes. For the first time in a long time, she realized she actually missed something about this place.

Tired and sweaty and happy, they finally reached the amusement park rides at the other end of the street. It was getting late, so their plan was to go on a few rides, get snow cones for themselves and treats for Vance, then go home.

But that's when Sawyer appeared, in khakis and a polo, winding his way toward them. Julia would have quickly steered Emily away and lost him if Emily hadn't seen him first and said, "There's Sawyer!" as if he were a rare and colorful bird they had to stand still to watch.

No one could deny that he *was* a sight to behold. But the muscles in her shoulders bunched and tightened as he approached. She'd been purposely avoiding him since last Tuesday, trying to devise a plan. She didn't know what to do without her animosity toward him. It had been her constant companion for years, and now that he'd broken through that, now that she'd made the decision to tell him about what had really happened all those years ago, she felt too vulnerable. She was walking a high wire without a net, and that kiss proved just how easily she could fall.

As he walked toward them, he gave Julia a look so hot she was almost embarrassed. Contrary to this look, however, the first words out of his mouth were, "I hope you're happy. My navigation system has been trying to take me to Frank's Toilet World all week."

Emily laughed, and Julia said, "Sorry."

"I get the feeling you *like* pointing me in the wrong direction." Before she could respond, he turned to Emily and said, "Are you having a good time?"

"We've had a great day," Emily said.

"We won't be staying much longer," Julia added. "We were about to take in a few rides, then go home."

He chose to interpret that as an invitation rather than a brush-off. Sawyer never had been good with rejection. It happened so rarely to him. "Great, then I'll join you."

"We don't want to keep you," Julia said. "Surely you're here with someone."

"I came alone, if that's what you're asking. I met up with Stella earlier, but then her entourage got too big. Stella is like a comet collecting space debris as she passes."

That made Emily laugh again, but Julia, more curious than she wanted to be ever since Sawyer had told her he'd once slept with Stella, asked seriously, "You didn't want to be a part of Stella's comet tail?"

"I was suddenly distracted by another heavenly body," he said, meeting her eyes.

Emily cleared her throat. "I'm sure you two want to be alone. Why don't you go on a ride together? I'd like to walk around by myself for a while, anyway."

Julia tore her eyes off Sawyer. "I don't think

that's a good idea, Em," she said, and actually put a hand on her shoulder, trying to keep her there.

"Why not?" Emily asked.

"Yes, Julia," Sawyer said, smiling. "Why not?

"Because I told your grandfather I'd keep an eye on you."

"I'll be fine."

"But . . ."

"Julia," Emily said reasonably, "I'm seventeen, not four."

Julia knew she wasn't going to win this one. "Meet me by the bandstand in one hour. One hour."

Emily kissed Julia's cheek. It was an unexpected gesture from her, a sweet, daughterly thing to do. "Thanks."

"One hour," Julia called after her as she watched the crowd swallow Emily. She had an overwhelming urge to drag her back, to protect her from everything that had hurt her so much as a teenager.

She finally turned back to Sawyer, who had his brows raised.

"She's been looking for an excuse to get away from me. Win Coffey has been eyeing her all afternoon. And I've seen her watching him."

"It was inevitable," Sawyer said. "Those two were going to have magnets attached to each other no matter what. The lure of the forbidden."

"I don't want her to get hurt. She's been through so much already."

"You really care about her, don't you? Nothing has happened yet. And Win is a pretty good kid. But if he does hurt her, he'll have me to contend with. Now," he said, leaning in slightly, putting his face close to hers, "let's talk about last Tuesday."

"I have a better idea," she said. "Let's go in the fun house, instead."

Sawyer looked confused. She couldn't blame him. "That's a better idea?"

"It's the fun house. Who doesn't love the fun house?" she said as she walked over to the small structure. It sounded ridiculous, even to her. But talking about last Tuesday was too far ahead of her plans. He wanted her. She'd known that since she came back. But there was the little matter of telling him about their daughter first. That was going to change everything.

Sawyer followed her and bought their tickets. When they entered, the undulating floor threw her off balance and she fell back against him. He took her hand and pulled her across the room. Many kids chose to stay in that room and ride the wooden waves, so when Julia and Sawyer tripped into the hall of mirrors, they were the only ones there.

She had to hold out her hands to make her way forward. Which was the walkway and which was just reflection? Which was the real Julia? She turned quickly when Sawyer disappeared from behind her.

"Where did you go?" she called.

"I'm not sure," he called back.

She turned and tried to follow his voice. She almost walked into a mirror, then followed the corner of that mirror to the corridor she thought he'd taken. The strobe lights didn't help. It was like they were in a psychedelic ice cave. And the frantic music in the room sounded like a heartbeat.

"If you want me to say I'm sorry for kissing you, I will," Sawyer said. She caught sight of him, then he disappeared again. "But I won't mean it. I'm sorry for a lot of things, but not that."

There! There he was again! No, he moved. "Stand still so I can find you," she said. "I don't want you to say you're sorry. It's just . . . I'm leaving soon. Nothing is going to change that. If you can accept that, then . . ."

Peals of laughter came from the next room. "Then . . . what?" Sawyer asked. "I can kiss you again?"

"That's not what I meant. There's a lot you don't know right now." She turned another corner, only to find herself in a dead end that looked like the mirrors in a department store dressing room. She backed out.

"It's starting to make sense," Sawyer said. "I even put the idea in your head, didn't I? 'Live a little, since you only have six months left here.' Or was this your plan all along, wait until a few months before you left, and then have one last hurrah?"

She stopped in her tracks, stung. How had this gone so wrong so fast? She was trying to do something good. "You think I'm capable of that?"

"You're capable of leaving for eighteen years without so much as a look back. Do you regret that at all?" His voice was moving away.

She charged forward, determined to catch up to him. "I wasn't the one who barreled ahead without looking back. And how do you know I didn't look back? Were you looking? No, you weren't. And you have no idea what my regrets are, Sawyer Alexander, so don't go there."

"You're right. I don't. You never shared them with me. You wanted them all to yourself. But what you're saying is the only way you can do this is if it's temporary. The only way you can let me in is knowing you get to leave me at a certain time. No strings. No dealing with our complicated past."

"Where are you?" she yelled in frustration.

"I have news for you. You can't have temporary. As a matter of fact, you're nowhere near where I want you to be."

"What does that mean?"

"Stay in Mullaby, Julia, and find out." She heard the squeak of a door opening, then closing.

"Sawyer? Sawyer!" It took a few minutes for her to make her way out. She went through the door and found herself in the rolling barrel. She ran through it, then through the air jets, but when she was finally outside again—the festival air textured like cotton candy—he was nowhere to be found.

What she'd been *trying* to say was she didn't think it was a good idea to pursue a relationship in light of what she had to tell him. He might hate her after she told him. She didn't mean she wanted a fling with him. But he *thought* she meant that, and seemed very eager to turn the tables. And for what? Just to have his way? Temporary, whether she meant it or not, should have been a dream come true for him. Instead, he insinuated that she couldn't have him unless it was by his rules. Unless she stayed.

Did he honestly think that stringing her along would work?

She thought he'd give her forever once, and look how well that turned out.

She walked down the street toward the bandstand, huffing with indignation. This was good. The animosity was back. She didn't owe him anything. She could just walk away now. Nothing more needed to be said.

Oh, God. If only she meant that.

If only he hadn't kissed her.

If only he hadn't told her . . .

Julia had barely made it out of the amusement ride area when she heard, "Julia! Jooooooooolia!"

She turned and saw Beverly walk up to her with tiny clips of her high-heeled sandals. Her husband, Bud Dale, was walking beside her, looking like a pack mule as he carried all her bags.

"Beverly," Julia said in flat acknowledgment. Then she turned to Beverly's husband. "I haven't seen you in a while, Bud. How are you?"

"I'm doing real well, Julia. You're real nice for askin'." There was something about the way he said that. It gave Julia pause. It was something her father would say, in that same good-ol'-boy kind of way. Beverly had left Julia's father, but then married a man just like him.

"I have a big surprise for you," Beverly said.

"What is it?"

"I don't have it with me now," she said, which Julia found hard to believe, considering how many shopping bags Bud was holding for her. "But I'll come by to see you tomorrow around lunchtime, okay? I'm so excited about it."

"Sure." Julia started to turn. "See you later."

"Why do you have to act this way, Julia?" Beverly asked, putting her hands on her hips. "Why are you always so *unhappy*? It's not an attractive quality. Why don't you spruce yourself up a little? Take that awful streak out of your hair. Smile at men, show a little skin." Beverly adjusted herself, pulling at the low V of her shirt. "Oh, I know you don't like to show your scars, but once you're in bed with a man, it's not your arms he'll be looking at, if you catch my meaning."

"Thanks for your input. Goodbye, Bud."

"Good seein' you, Julia," he said as she walked away.

"I always tried to be a mother to her," she heard Beverly say. "You know, share my expertise. But I think there's something wrong with her that can't be fixed."

Julia fought with herself, trying not to turn around and confront Beverly. Beverly had been no kind of mother to her. Julia kept walking, telling herself she wouldn't have to put up with this, or with Sawyer, for very long.

Between the two of them, was it any wonder she was unhappy? She'd be fine as soon as she was back in Baltimore. Though she couldn't remember ever being incredibly happy there, she knew opening her bakery was going to change things.

And at least she wouldn't be here.

EMILY WALKED around slowly, surrounded by the hot mist from food vendors and the tinny horn music from the kiddie rides. She was trying not to look like she was looking for him. There was a chance Win didn't mean he wanted to spend any actual time with her at the festival when he'd asked if he would see her here. But there'd been no opportunity to find out for sure until now.

She'd seen him several times that day, just passing glimpses before Julia pulled her away, or his father distracted him. Emily was so relieved that Sawyer had come up to them when he did. It had given her the perfect excuse to go out on her own, although Julia didn't seem as happy with the idea of being alone with Sawyer as Emily thought she would be.

Barely five minutes later, as she was heading to the information booth where she'd last seen Win as he was giving out directions to visitors, she felt a familiar warm hand on her arm.

She turned around and smiled.

Win had taken off his jacket and tie and his sleeves were rolled up. He'd lost the boater hat, too. He managed to look Caribbean cool, his white button-down billowing every time the wind picked up. His eyes were intense and green as he looked down on her.

"Hi" was her brilliant opening line. She couldn't help it. Being this close to him flustered her.

"Hello," he said.

"Have you noticed there's a conspiracy to keep us at least twenty feet away from each other at all times? Who would have thought being friends would be this hard?"

He waved his hand forward, indicating they should walk. "I think that's the difference between us," he said, looking over his shoulder, distracted. "I knew how hard it would be going in."

"So you get the badge of courage?"

"I'm sorry," he said. "I didn't mean it like that. I'm glad to finally spend some time with you."

Slightly mollified, she said, "I wish I could figure you out, Win."

That made a side of his mouth lift into a smile.

"If you only knew how refreshing it is to hear that."

"Oh, come on. You mean everyone has figured you out but me?"

He shrugged, making the fabric of his shirt wrinkle at his shoulders. "Everyone in Mullaby, at least."

"Gee, as if I didn't feel like such an oddball already."

"See, that's exactly what I mean. You live in such a strange town, and yet *you* feel odd."

As they walked, their arms touched as they were jostled by the crowd. She liked the unintentional nature of it. Everything else about Win was so deliberate. "Well, I'm glad I could shake things up for you," she said, which made him laugh.

They'd only been walking for a few minutes before he stopped and led her to a short queue. "Let's go on this ride," he said suddenly.

"Why this one?" she asked, following him. Being with him felt like a game sometimes, only she didn't know the rules. Or who was winning.

"Because it's closest," he said. "And my dad is nearby."

Emily looked back, trying to find Morgan Coffey, but she couldn't see him. Win paid for their tickets and they crossed the deck to the Ferris wheel. They took the next available seat and the attendant placed the safety bar across them.

Win put his arm over the back of the seat behind

her and focused on the sky as the wheel slowly lifted them up. Emily, however, looked down at the crowd as it got smaller and smaller. She finally found his father. He was standing as still as stone, watching them with an expression made of ghosts and anger.

"He'll leave soon," Win said, still looking up at the dusky sky. "He won't want anyone knowing that it bothers him that we're together."

"You and your dad don't get along, do you?"

"We're alike in many ways. But we don't see eye to eye. For example, he's very attached to doing things the way they've always been done. I don't agree."

The Ferris wheel came to a stop two seats down from the top. "I've been thinking about you a lot this past week," she said, and it came out a lot more moony that she intended.

He lowered his gaze from the sky and met her eyes. His smile was mischievous. "Oh?"

"Not like that," she said, laughing. She stopped laughing when their seat swayed back and forth in the wind. She grabbed the safety bar in front of them. Of course *he* didn't seem afraid to be up this high. "I just can't get my mind around something."

"What is it?"

"You wouldn't happen to be a werewolf, would you?"

"Excuse me?" he said.

She slowly loosened her hold on the bar and

sat back. "There are only two reasons I can think of for why you don't come out at night: night blindness or werewolf."

"And you decided to go with werewolf?"

"It was a toss-up."

Win didn't answer for a few moments. He finally said, "It's tradition. It's gone on for centuries."

"Why?"

"That's a good question. I guess because that's what traditions do."

"Is this another thing you and your father don't see eye to eye on?"

The wheel started moving again. "Yes. But going against this tradition is a big deal." He turned to her. "Of all the things I'm going to tell you, you need to understand that the most."

She suddenly felt excited. "What things are you going to tell me?"

"Strange and wondrous things," he said in a dramatic voice, like he was narrating a book.

"And why? Why are you doing this?"

"I told you before, we have history."

"Technically, we don't," she pointed out. "Your uncle and my mother had history."

"History is a loop. We're exactly where they stood twenty years ago. What's theirs is ours, what's ours will become theirs."

"You've thought about this a lot."

"Yes, I have."

The wheel made one more rotation before stopping again. This time they were at the very top of the ride. Their seat creaked as it swung precariously back and forth. Emily grabbed the bar again.

Win smiled at her. "You're not afraid, are you?"

"Of course not. Are you?"

He looked out over the horizon. "I like seeing things from this perspective. I know what everything looks like from down there. I like seeing the possibilities of what's beyond that. What's beyond that loop I was talking about."

She didn't realize she was staring at him until he turned to stare back. The air around them suddenly changed. She was so close she could smell him, a hint of cologne, and she could see the perspiration collected in the indentation at the base of his throat. His eyes went to her lips. Something warm and desperate filled her body. She'd never felt anything like it. It felt like the entire universe would cease to exist if something didn't happen *right then*.

But the moment passed and his chest rose and fell as if taking a very deep breath of air. He moved his arm from the back of the seat.

After another rotation, the wheel stopped and the attendant unhooked the safety bar. They both got off the ride without a word and walked off the deck.

"I'm sorry, but I've got to go," he said.

She was still feeling strange, sort of buzzed and prickly. "Okay."

But he didn't leave. "My dad is around the corner, waiting," he explained. "I want to spare you whatever it is he might say."

"Okay."

And still he didn't go. "And it's going to get dark soon."

"And you don't want to grow fur and fangs in front of me," she said. "I get it."

His dark hair was curling in the humidity. He ran his hands through it. "No, I don't think you do."

"Then explain it to me. Tell me these strange and wondrous things."

That made him smile, like it was exactly what he wanted to hear, like he'd been planning this all along. "I will. Next time." He turned to leave.

"Wait," she called, and he stopped. "I need to ask you something."

"What is it?"

She decided to come right out and say it. "Do you blame me for what my mother did?"

"Of course not," he said immediately.

"But your father does."

He hesitated. "I can't speak for him."

"My grandfather told me that my mom got angry because the Coffeys wouldn't let her into their social circle, and that's why she did what she did."

"That's how the story goes," he said. His eyes bored into her with a sudden and intense curiosity.

She pushed her hair behind her ears, and his

eyes followed the movement. "I just want you to know that . . . I'm not mad."

"Excuse me?"

"That your family doesn't like me. I understand why. And I'm not mad."

"Oh, Emily," he said.

"What?"

"You're making this very hard."

"What? Leaving?"

"That too. Next time?"

She nodded. She liked that, the continuance, the anticipation. What would he do? What would he say? She was too enamored of him, too fascinated. But she couldn't seem to help it. She wanted to fit in here, and he made her feel like she did.

"Next time," she said as he walked away.

EMILY MET Julia by the bandstand as promised, and she could tell that both their moods had changed since they'd last been together. They bought Grandpa Vance a barbecue sandwich and a fried pickle, then headed home. Neither of them was particularly chatty.

Julia said a distracted goodbye when they reached Grandpa Vance's house. Emily watched her walk away. Something was definitely on her mind.

When Emily walked into the house, she knocked on the wall beside the accordion door to Vance's bedroom. "Grandpa Vance, I'm home."

When he opened the door, she caught her first glimpse of his bedroom, which had obviously once been the living room. The curtains were drawn over the windows to keep the heat out, but the light through the rust-colored material cast a glow of permanent sunset over the room. The room looked like it should smell stuffy, but there was actually a very faint scent of sweet perfume lingering in the air, as if a woman had left only moments before.

There were rows upon rows of photographs on the shelves on the far wall, older photos of the same woman, a pretty woman with blond hair and Emily's mother's smile. That must be her grandmother Lily. Where were the photos of her mother, she wondered. Did he have any?

She held up the foil-wrapped food. "I brought you some stuff from the festival."

"Wonderful! I think I'll eat in the kitchen. Will you join me?" He led the way. As soon as they reached the kitchen, Vance went directly to the laundry room. Emily heard the dryer door open, then close. Then Vance walked back out. "So, how did you like our little barbecue shindig?"

Emily smiled. "It wasn't little at all."

"What did you and Julia do?" He went to the breakfast nook and sat, absently rubbing his knees as if they ached.

"Wandered around. Ate too much. She bought me this T-shirt." Emily walked over to him and placed the food on the table, then sat opposite him.

She brought the T-shirt out of the small bag she'd been carrying.

"Ha! That's a good one," Vance said as he read what was on the shirt. "Did you see any kids your age?"

Emily hesitated before she said, "Just Win Coffey."

"Well, it is their festival," he said as he unwrapped his food and began to eat. "You need to meet some other people your age. As I recall, my friend Lawrence Johnson has a grandson . . . in middle school, I think."

Confused, Emily said, "Do you think he'd want me to babysit?"

"Yes, I guess that is a little young for you," Vance said. "It's only July. School doesn't start until next month, and you're going to get bored." He suddenly looked worried. "That friend of your mother's, Merry, said she would take care of getting you registered and your class credits transferred. Do you think I should check the school, just in case?"

Emily had been so focused on what was going on here, she hadn't given Merry much thought lately. That startled her. "Merry probably handled everything. She's very detail-oriented, just like Mom." Emily looked down to the T-shirt in her lap. "Mom helped found the school I went to. Did you know that?"

He nodded. "Merry and I had a long talk. Your

mother had a remarkable life. Merry told me a lot about you, too. She said you were involved in a lot of activities."

Emily shrugged. Her old life felt so bound and heavy now. "They were school requirements."

"I bet there are a lot of activities you can get involved in here. Lots of stuff you can do at night."

She knew what he was doing, being about as subtle as an eight-foot-tall man. He didn't want her associating with Win. She understood why. At the same time, she wondered if she could change this, if the reason she came here, in the whole scheme of things, was to make this right. Like her mother said, *Don't wait for the world to change.* She'd been thinking a lot lately about clues her mother might have given her over the years, either on purpose or unconsciously, about her time here, about lessons she'd learned. Who she'd become, Emily was beginning understand, was her penance. She'd hurt people when she was young. She'd saved them when she got older. But for all the good she'd done, she'd never thought it was enough. Her mother had never been satisfied.

After Grandpa Vance ate, he got up and threw the food wrappers away. Then he went back to the laundry room to check the dryer.

She couldn't stand it any longer. She had to know. When he came back out, she slid out of her seat in the breakfast nook and asked, "Why do you do that? Check the dryer so often?"

196

He laughed and gave her a sly look. "I was wondering when you'd ask," he said. He walked to the refrigerator and took out two green bottles of 7UP. He handed one to Emily. "I was a little uptight when Lily and I first married. I'd lived alone for quite a while before she moved in. Without realizing I was doing it, I would follow her around when she would do housework, to make sure it was done the way I'd always done it. The thing that bothered Lily the most was my checking the dryer after her to see if she'd left any clothes behind." He shook his head at the memory. "Because I'm so tall, I can't see that low into the dryer, so I just reach down and feel. One day, after she'd walked out with a basket of laundry, I went in and stuck my hand in the dryer . . . and felt something cold and slimy. She'd set a frog from the backyard in the dryer for me to find! I jerked my hand out so fast that I fell down. Then out jumps the frog. I watched him hop from the room, past Lily's shoes. She was standing in the doorway, laughing. Well, I learned my lesson. Over the years, she'd tell me to go check the dryer as a joke, and I'd always find a small gift from her." Her twisted the top off his bottle and took a drink. "After she died, I just kept checking. I don't know why. It's not like I ever find anything. But it makes me think of her. And when I get worried or anxious about something, I go check, just in case she wants to tell me something."

"I think that's sweet, Grandpa Vance," Emily said. "I wish I'd known her."

"I do, too. She would have liked you."

They said good night at the staircase, and Vance went back into his room. Emily made it halfway up the staircase before she stopped. She hesitated, then walked back down and went to the laundry room.

She studied the dryer for a moment, even going so far as to lean over it to see what was behind it. Before she knew what she was doing, her hand went to the handle and she quickly opened the door, jumping back as if something inside might fly out at her.

She cautiously peered in. Nothing was there.

She almost laughed at herself as she walked out. What had possessed her to do that?

What sign was *she* looking for?

HOURS LATER Emily slowly opened her eyes, not sure what had awakened her. She took a deep breath. When she exhaled, in her sleep-addled mind, the air came out as blue as smoke. She stared at the ceiling and it gradually came to her. Something was wrong. The room was normally brighter than this.

When she'd gone to sleep, light from the moon was shining in through the open balcony doors, sending rays as pale as cream into the room. She turned her head on the pillow to see that the balcony doors she'd left open were now closed, and the curtains had been drawn over them.

Her heart suddenly gave a single hard thud of surprise and her scalp tightened, which felt like every hair was on end. *Someone had been in her room.* She reached under her pillow and turned off her MP3 player, then she slowly sat up on her elbows.

She knew it was him. His presence *felt* different, different from anyone she'd ever known. She could feel the lingering warmth of him still in the air.

She pulled the earbuds out of her ears and got up and went quickly to the light switch. When she flicked it on, the chandelier bathed the room in cobwebby light.

But no one was there.

From across the room, she saw a piece of paper peeking out from the curtains. The twin doors had been shut with a note tucked between them. She hurried over and pulled the note out.

I'm sorry I had to leave the festival. I didn't want to. Will you spend the day with me? Meet me on the boardwalk at Piney Woods Lake this morning. —Win.

Emily immediately swung open the doors and stepped out on the balcony, looking around.

"Win?"

Nothing. The only sounds were the katydids and the papery rustling of leaves in the wind.

Her heart was still thumping, heavy and fast, but not so much from fear now as an incredible sense of anticipation. It had been a long time since she'd felt anything like this. It had been months since she'd looked forward to anything—food, birthdays, weekends. He made her remember how it felt.

The edge of her nightgown was fluttering against her legs, and the air around her was charged with energy. She didn't want to move. She didn't want to let go of this feeling.

A few minutes later, she heard an engine turn over. The lights of Julia's truck, parked at the curb in front of her house, suddenly sprang to life. Emily watched the truck pull away and drive down the street.

She guessed she wasn't the only one who wasn't going to sleep that night.

Chapter 12

*W*hen Sawyer opened the door to his townhouse, he was irritated, as anyone would be if they were forced out of bed at dark-thirty by the incessant ringing of a doorbell. The neighborhood had better be on fire.

The door flew open and hit the wall as he flicked on the porch light.

Julia took her hand away from the doorbell, and the grating shriek inside his house immediately stopped.

He blinked a few times. "Julia?" he asked, just to be sure.

"I need to talk to you."

"Now?" He wasn't at his best.

She rolled her eyes. "Yes, now."

He took a good long look at her. She hadn't changed clothes. She was wearing the same faded jeans and embroidered white peasant blouse she'd been wearing at the festival. He should have stayed there with her, but he'd been angry. She thought he only wanted a piece of her, that he would accept a fling. While he'd certainly had his share of flings, most of which he'd greatly enjoyed, he wanted to be nobler than that with Julia. *And she wouldn't let him.* "Are you drunk?" he asked.

"No, I am not drunk. I'm mad."

"Oh, good, because for a moment there I thought it was going to be something unusual." He stepped back. "Come in." It was an automatic gesture. He didn't think anything of it until she walked past him into his darkened living room. That's when it hit him. She was in his house. Exactly where he wanted her to be. And he had no idea what to do next.

The only light came from his kitchen, where he kept the hood light over his oven on at night. She looked around, nodding slightly to herself, as if his space was exactly what she expected it to be, like there was a fine, crisp scent of privilege here that she didn't like.

"Is this about the big thing you wanted to tell me?" he asked, slightly afraid that it was. One big thing left to tell him, and then she wouldn't want anything more to do with him?

She turned to face him, her brows lowered. "What?"

"Last week, you gave me a cake, told me you started baking because of me, then said there was some big thing you were going to tell me later. Is this later?"

"No, this has nothing to do with that. Why would I be mad about that?"

He sighed. "I don't know, Julia. When it comes to you, it's all guesswork."

She began to pace. "I was fine here until you went all humble on me. And you almost had me, too. I almost trusted you." She made a scoffing sound. "And you accuse *me* of being conniving."

"What are you talking about?"

"I'm talking about what you said today."

He rubbed the side of his face. The blond stubble of his beard made a scratchy sound. "Refresh my memory."

"You said that I'm only letting you in because I'm planning to leave. *And then you walked away from me.*"

"Ah." He let his hand drop. "That."

"I wasn't saying that at all, which I would have told you if you'd stuck around. But it doesn't matter that it wasn't what I meant. Because, so what?"

He was beginning to think it wasn't his sleepy mind after all. She really was making no sense. "Excuse me?"

"So what if I was only letting you in because I'm planning to leave. Why would that matter to you? You've been trying to get into my pants ever since I came back, and you were going to let something like my leaving get in your way? It didn't get in your way last time."

His head suddenly felt hot. She'd struck a nerve. "For the record, you know as well as I do that I could get into your pants at any time." He took a step toward her, so close his chest grazed her breasts. "Because I know exactly how to do that."

"So do it now," she said, obviously trying to be brave, but her voice faltered a little.

"I want in here, too." He put his finger to her temple.

"You are there."

"What about here?" He put his hand on her chest, over her heart. Her heart was racing. Was it anger? Fear? Lust?

She suddenly took a step back. "You're not going to do that to me again."

"What?"

"Weasel your way into my heart. Charm me and

make me think it's for real, that it's forever. It took years to get over it last time. You are *not* going to insinuate forever to me again. You're not going to promise me anything, and I'm not promising you. So that 'Stay, because you're nowhere near where I want you to be' crap isn't going to work. Do you know how much easier it would have been if you had just promised me one night? That night? Do realize how much I hated you for making me think you loved me?"

"Julia . . ."

"No. Promise me one night," she said. "Don't promise to love me. Don't ask me to stay."

To hell with nobility. He reached for her and kissed her. It was all at once passionate, as if there was too much in him to contain. He was immediately swept up in it. It took no effort, the difference between swimming on your own and being washed away in a flood.

His hands went to the hem of her shirt and slowly pushed it up. When his hands brushed over her bare breasts, her back arched. He broke their kiss. Her fingers automatically tightened in his hair, as if wanting him back. "Jesus, you came here without a bra on," he said.

He backed her against the wall, and soon her shirt was over her head. She started moving restlessly against him. It made him groan. He clamped a hand onto her hip and surged against her. She met his rhythm flawlessly.

He reached down and unbuttoned her jeans, and she tried to help him push them down while not breaking their kiss, but their lips kept separating. Finally he simply used his foot to slide them the rest of the way down, and she stepped out of them.

"You want one night, I'll give it to you," he said as he picked her up and carried her to the couch. "But it's going to be one hell of a night."

He stood over her, staring down at her so hungrily that she made an attempt to cover herself. His hands went to the waistband of his pajama bottoms and pushed them down, not taking his eyes off of her. He put one knee on the couch beside her. She swallowed and put her hand up to his bare chest. "Wait, Sawyer."

He hung his head, sucking in breaths. "What are you doing to me, Julia?"

"I meant, wait because I have to get the condoms out of my jeans pocket."

He lifted his head, surprised. "I wasn't lying. I can't have kids."

"Are you sure?"

"I'm sure." He got up anyway, completely unself-conscious, and went to her jeans. He dug out the condoms and made quick work of putting one on.

"No more waiting," he said as he covered her body with his.

"No more waiting."

It had never been like this with anyone else.

They held on to each other as if the force of their bodies coming together could make everything that had ever separated them disappear. And it did, for a short period of time, time he wished he could stop so he could live inside it for the rest of his life.

Afterward, breath gone, clinging to each other so hard they would leave marks, Sawyer, whose head was buried in Julia's neck, managed to say, "Contrary to my lamentable lack of restraint just now, I have actually learned a few things since I was sixteen."

She gave a sudden laugh.

"And as soon as I have the strength to get up, I'm taking you to my bedroom and showing you."

IT WAS morning, but still dark in his bedroom when she woke up. Sawyer watched as she blinked a few times and turned her head on the pillow to find him staring at her.

Her hair was rumpled, the pink streak curling around her ear. She took a deep, defeated breath. "I thought I had everything figured out."

"Do you think promising you another night might clear things up?"

She smiled, but didn't answer.

He brushed one finger lightly against her forearm. He saw the moment she realized he was following the lines of her scars. She immediately pulled her arm away. He pulled it back.

206

"Why did you do this to yourself?" he asked.

She watched him as he watched his finger trace the lines. "It was my way of dealing with the depression and isolation I felt. I didn't know how to cope, and all my anger was turned inward, so this is what I did. Don't think I'm naturally this enlightened. That's years of therapy speaking."

He met her eyes. "Do you ever think of doing it again?"

"No. In case you hadn't noticed, I'm very good at expressing my anger these days." She shifted slightly, then winced a little.

"Are you okay?"

She cleared her throat. "It's . . . been a while."

Was it wrong that that made him happy? He didn't care. It did. He'd spent a lot of time wondering about what she was doing in Baltimore, thinking about who she was with. He knew so little about that part of her life. "Why didn't you come back to Mullaby, Julia?"

"I didn't think there was anything left for me." She rolled her head back on the pillow and stared at the ceiling.

"Didn't you ever get homesick?"

"I'm homesick all the time," she said, still not looking at him. "I just don't know where home is. There's this promise of happiness out there. I know it. I even feel it sometimes. But it's like chasing the moon—just when I think I have it, it disappears into the horizon. I grieve and try to move on, but then the damn thing comes back the next night, giving me hope of catching it all over again."

He'd never heard her so raw and honest. Julia, who always kept her feelings to herself. "Is that the big thing you were going to tell me?"

"No."

He groaned. "You're killing me. Is it something good?"

"Yes."

He put his hand on her thigh and started moving his way up. "Better than last night?"

"There's no comparison." She put her hand on his, stopping the movement. "What time is it?"

He lifted himself on his elbow and looked over to the clock on the nightstand. "A little after nine."

She hesitated. "In the morning?"

"Yes."

She gasped and jumped out of the bed. She went to the heavy curtains and threw them open. Morning light immediately cut into the dark room. When the spots left his vision, he found himself staring at her naked body, silhouetted in the window. He was riveted. She made his stomach tight, his head light.

"I can't believe it's morning! Why didn't you tell me? What kind of curtains are these?" She grabbed the offending material and looked at it closely. "I thought it was night!"

"They're insulated light-blockers. I'd be blinded every morning if I didn't have them." He sat up against his pillows and put his hands behind his head. "I really enjoy this side of you, but I think you're giving my neighbors the best view. Why don't you turn around?"

She quickly stepped away from the window and covered herself with one of the curtain panels. "I can't believe I just flashed your neighbors. On a Sunday morning."

"I know I saw the face of God."

"I've got to go," she said, eyeing the door.

"No."

"I have to make the day's cakes at the restaurant. I'm so late. I'm usually there and gone by now. Where are my clothes?" She looked around, then said, "Oh, downstairs." And she darted, naked, from his room.

He smiled and got up. He took his robe from the back of his door and put it on as he walked down the stairs after her.

She was quick. She already had on her jeans and her shoes, and was pulling her shirt over her head. By the time her head poked through the collar, he was there, backing her against the wall by the door.

"We're back where we started. I think this is a sign that we need to do it again."

"If you let me go, I'll bake you a cake."

"Vixen."

Suddenly there was a knock at the door, directly to the right, which startled Julia so much she let out a small scream.

Sawyer winced and rubbed his ear.

"Who is that?" she whispered.

"I don't know."

"Don't answer it. Maybe they'll go away."

"And call the police because there was a woman screaming in here. What's the problem? You don't want people to know we've been together?" He turned and went to the door before she could answer, because he was afraid of what that answer might be. Even after last night, she was still water in his hands. He didn't know how to hold on.

Sawyer opened the door. When he saw who was standing there, he thought, *Oh, damn.* This wasn't going to help things at all.

"Hi, Sawyer," Holly said as she walked in. "Was that you screaming like a girl?"

Holly stopped when she saw Julia. There was an awkward moment when the three of them, cramped in the small space by the door, didn't say anything, just stared at one another.

"Holly," Sawyer finally said, "you remember Julia Winterson?"

"Of course," Holly said, giving Sawyer a pointed look before turning to Julia and smiling. "It's nice to see you, Julia."

"You too. I'm sorry to run, but I'm late." And in seconds, she was gone. Again.

Sawyer closed the door and turned to his ex-wife. "I forgot you were coming by."

Holly kissed him on the cheek and walked through his living room to his kitchen and began to make coffee. He followed her, remembering the feeling he had when he first asked Holly to be his girlfriend in sixth grade, that intense I'll-finally-get-to-hold-her-hand feeling. She was his best friend all through school. He valued her. He respected her. But he didn't know if he was ever in love with her. That night with Julia on the football field should have told him that, but he'd been too afraid to give up on the future he'd planned.

He was the one who had ended the marriage. Holly would have stayed once they'd found out he couldn't have kids. In fact, she'd become almost manically determined to stick it out. She'd brought home information on adoption and tried to be enthusiastic. Kids were an integral part of their plan, but he realized she wanted them so much because what they had together wasn't enough. It never had been.

"You finally did it," Holly said when he walked into the kitchen. She was scooping coffee grounds out of the can. "I can't believe it."

Sawyer pulled out a stool and sat at the counter. "What are you talking about?"

"Don't play dumb with me." She looked over her shoulder with a grin. She looked good. Happy. Her hair was pulled back into a ponytail, revealing that her face was fuller, rounding out her normally sharp cheekbones. She'd put on weight. "I know you too well. You've had a thing for her since we were kids. And you finally got her."

Sawyer sighed. "I'm not so sure about that."

Holly's smile disappeared. "Oh, hell. I didn't . . ."

"No, it's not your fault. You look fantastic, by the way."

"Are you really okay with this? With me getting married again? With this?" She put her hand to her stomach.

"I'm happy for you, Holly. I truly am."

She snorted and turned back to the coffee. "I think you're only saying that because you got some last night."

Sawyer slid off the stool and walked to his office. "I'll get the papers for you to sign."

LIQUID MORNING light was rippling through the open balcony doors when Emily woke up. She had no idea what time it was, but she felt she'd only been asleep for minutes.

The note.

She turned quickly to the bedside table. The note was still there, where she'd left it.

She picked it up and stared at it. She was tempted to even put it to her nose.

Was she going to do it? Was she going to meet him?

Win said he didn't blame her for what her mother had done, but how could she know for sure? What were his motives? She wouldn't know until this had played itself out.

Her mother was the bravest person she had ever known, yet even she hadn't been able to face down her past.

So Emily would.

She would do something her mother couldn't do. In order to find her place here, she had to set herself apart from who her mother had been, but she also had to try to make it right. How exactly she was going to do that, she didn't know. There was a nagging part of her that suspected Win might know, that his interest in her wasn't as simple as he wanted it to seem. But then, her interest in him was pretty complicated, too.

She thought about the history loop he'd talked about. Here she was in the same place her mother had been, at about the same age, and involved with the Coffeys in a way no one approved of, just like last time. There had to be a reason for it.

She got up, the note still in her hand, and walked to her dresser for shorts and a tank top. She was getting used to averting her eyes to avoid looking at the frenzied butterfly wallpaper, getting used to the soft fluttering sound it occasionally gave off. Getting used to it meant she was fitting in, according to Julia.

Either that, or she was officially going crazy.

When she reached the dresser, though, she suddenly realized there wasn't any sound that morning. She looked up and took a surprised step back. The butterfly wallpaper was now gone. It had been replaced by a moody, breathless wall-paper of silver, sprinkled with tiny white dots that looked like stars. It made her feel an odd sense of anticipation, like last night. Grandpa Vance couldn't have come in last night and done this.

Did it really change on its own?

It was beautiful, this wallpaper. It made the room look like living in a cloud. She put her hand against the wall by her dresser. It was soft, like velvet. How could her mother not have told her a room like this existed? She'd never mentioned it. Not even in a bedtime story.

She dressed quickly, distracted, and went down-stairs. Thankfully, Grandpa Vance had already left for breakfast, so she wrote him a note telling him she'd be at the lake.

She didn't mention who she was meeting there.

Once on the sidewalk, she was about to get in her car when she heard her name being called in the morning quiet. Already jittery, she jumped in sur-prise and dropped her car keys. She turned quickly to see Stella walking toward her from next door. She looked strangely overdressed for that time of morning, in a strapless red dress and heels. Her wide face had fading blotches of makeup on it, and her exotic eyes were tired. She looked like she'd had a bad night. Or maybe a very good one. Emily couldn't decide which.

"Have you seen Julia?" Stella asked as Emily

knelt to pick up her keys. "I just went by J's Barbecue and she wasn't there."

Emily stood. "I haven't seen her since yesterday. But I did hear her leave in her truck around one o'clock this morning."

Stella looked confused. "I wonder where she went."

Emily shrugged. She tried to act casual, like she wasn't doing anything wrong. Which, of course, she wasn't. What was the matter with her? Why was she so nervous?

"Julia almost never uses her truck, and she never goes out that late. I'm worried about her." Stella started picking at her red fingernail polish. She shifted her weight to one hip and asked, "Do you think she's been acting weird lately?"

"Only around Sawyer."

"Hmm. Something's on her mind. If I get enough wine in her, I can usually get her to talk. But I think she's onto me about that now."

Emily looked over her shoulder anxiously, half expecting to see Grandpa Vance coming home. "She hasn't said anything to me."

"Well, if you see her, tell her I'm looking for her." Stella nodded to the Oldsmobile at the curb. "Where are you going at this time of morning?"

"To the lake. What about you?"

"Oh, I'm just getting in," Stella said, then paused. "Crap. I can't believe I said that to you. Erase that. I'm not setting a very good example. Crap. Just . . . do as I say, not as I do."

That made Emily laugh as she got in her car. Stella walked back to her house, taking off her heels and shaking her head to herself.

There was so little traffic at that time of morning that Emily arrived at Piney Woods Lake in record time. The parking lot was nearly empty. She parked and turned off the ignition, then sat in silence while the engine ticked as it cooled. She knew she was too early, but she'd wanted to leave before Grandpa Vance got home. She didn't want to lie to his face. She didn't know if he would understand why she was doing this.

Finally she got out of the car. The murky morning air was so heavy that it beaded on her skin as she walked to the boardwalk and sat on one of the benches overlooking the lake. There were very few people there. She propped her feet on the railing while watching the fog roll off the water. Some of the lake houses had their lights on, but not many.

She heard footsteps approach on the boardwalk behind her, then Win appeared by the bench. She stared up at him, not knowing what to say. She had no idea he would be here this early, too. He waited a moment, then he sat beside her and put his feet on the railing beside hers. He stared intently at the water as if he would miss something important if he looked away. He had a strong, angular profile. Austere, proud, full of secrets. She wanted in. She wanted to know those secrets.

Was this how her mother felt? She wondered if there was a curse, one that impossibly attracted the women of her family to the men of his.

Yet here she was. Still doing this.

"Come to my family's lake house and have breakfast with me," he finally said.

"How long have you been waiting?"

"A while. I didn't want to miss you." He took a deep breath, then stood. "I'm glad you came." He held out his hand to her.

It didn't take long for her to accept it.

Chapter 13

They walked down the empty beach, then Win led Emily up the steps to the large deck of his family's lake house. He gestured for her to sit in one of the Adirondack chairs. She did, pulling her legs up and wrapping her arms around them.

She relaxed this stance only when Penny, the housekeeper, came out and served them frittatas. Penny was sixty-three years old, widowed, and extremely set in her ways. But she had a soft spot for Win, and Win adored her. When he was a little boy, he used to think of Penny and the lake house as a single entity. He'd thought she sat alertly on a stool in the kitchen all day and night, waiting for his family to visit so she could cook for them. The first time he'd seen her outside the context of the lake house, on one of her days off, he'd been downtown with his mother. He'd seen Penny walk down the street and he'd thought she'd escaped, so he'd yelled at his mom to catch her and bring her back. He'd been absolutely hysterical. His limited understanding at the time had been that, because of who he was, he couldn't leave Mullaby, but other people could. They could leave and never come back. And that had petrified him.

He and Emily ate breakfast in a silence that wasn't entirely comfortable. He made her nervous, and she made him feel off balance. It felt like too much, like he was taking more than he should. But he couldn't seem to help it. He'd spent his life accepting what his father told him he could never change, and forcing himself not to covet the freedom other people had. Things had to change. He couldn't go on following rules that were made for a different time. It all made sense when he met Emily. She could make this right. She could take away this stigma. If Dulcie Shelby's daughter, of all people, could accept him for who he was, then his family would have to take notice. Emily was the first step to a whole new way of life.

At this point, he couldn't even consider the possibility that he was wrong about this. He had to be right. He *had* to be.

After breakfast, they sat side by side on the Adirondack chairs, quietly watching the sun burn the morning fog away. The beach was slowly filling with people, and the noise was beginning to swell.

"Are you out here a lot in the summer?" Emily finally asked, watching a boat zoom across the lake, leaving a trail of churning water that looked like soda foam.

He'd been biting his tongue, waiting for her to say something, not wanting to rush her. "My family uses this house all year round. It's a home away from home. It drives Penny crazy, though. She likes to keep to a strict schedule, and we always throw her off it by showing up unexpectedly, like I did this morning."

"I get the feeling she doesn't mind. I think she adores you." She looked over to him with a smile that made his chest feel full. He was manipulating her. He knew that. But for the first time, he realized how easily she could be doing the same to him. He needed to be her friend to make this work. He never expected to have these other feelings. One well-placed smile and he forgot what he was going to say. All he could think was how different she was than he thought she would be, after all the stories he'd heard about her mother. She was striking and sweet . . . and had the most interesting hair. It always looked like a gust of wind was hiding in there, waiting to blow out. It was so endearingly quirky.

In the silence that followed, her smile faded and her hands went to her hair. "Do I have something on my head?"

"No, sorry. I was just thinking about your hair."

She gave him an odd look. "You were thinking about my hair?"

This was the same hiccup he'd felt on the Ferris wheel with her. He couldn't lose focus. "Yes. No. I mean, I was wondering if you ever wore it down."

She shook her head. "It's in that weird growing-out stage right now."

"How short was it before?"

"Really short. My mom wore her hair short, so I wore mine short, too. But I started growing it out a little over a year ago."

"What made you stop wanting to be like her?"

"I've never stopped wanting to be like her. She was a wonderful person," she said vehemently. Then she turned back to the water. "It was just a lot to live up to."

This wasn't working. They had to shake some of this awkwardness off. "Let's go for a walk," he said as he stood.

They left their shoes by their chairs and went back down the deck steps. They walked close to the water and got their feet wet. They didn't talk much, but that was okay. Walking together, their strides in rhythm, getting used to each other, was enough.

When they reached the cove, Emily looked toward the grotto where his sister's birthday party had been held. There were two elderly couples sitting on folding chairs there today, away from the crowds and out of the sun. He knew what she was going to do before she took the first step.

Without a word, Emily left him and walked away from the water, toward the trees. He hesitated a moment before following her. She passed the elderly couples and went to the tree where her mother's and his uncle's initials had been carved. Win stopped to say hello to the elderly couples, to put their minds at ease, because they were looking at Emily strangely, then he went to stand by her.

The past few months of her life had been marked by a chaos he could only imagine. Looking at her like this, he could see her grief. He could see how alone she felt with it. But he understood that. He knew about things you couldn't tell other people because they had no basis for comparison. Because they simply wouldn't understand.

"Will the kids at Mullaby High know about my mom? About who she was here?" Emily finally asked, staring at the tree.

"If their parents tell them. You probably got the worst of it from my dad. I wouldn't worry about Mullaby High. It's not that bad." He hated seeing her like this. He wanted to distract her. "Tell me about your old school. Do you miss it? The website made it seem very . . . intense." That was putting it mildly. Roxley School for Girls was so full of righteous, politically correct indignation that a person could get a nosebleed just by reading the literature.

She shrugged. "After my mom died, I wanted to find some sort of comfort in the school, but I couldn't. There was just this *legacy*. More than ever, people there wanted me to fill my mom's shoes, and I couldn't. Ironic, isn't it, that I come here and the same thing has happened, just in a different way. And I don't know which is worse, trying to live up to her name, or trying to live it down."

"What about your friends there?"

"I started having panic attacks after my mother died, and I didn't want people to see me having them, so I started spending a lot of time by myself."

He suddenly thought of her sitting on the bench downtown with her head down. He'd been watching her for a while that morning, and he'd seen the moment something was wrong, the way she'd stopped short on the sidewalk, the color draining from her face. It had been alarming, and had forced him to approach her, when he hadn't planned to at all. And that had changed everything. "Were you having a panic attack the first day we met?"

She nodded.

"What brings them on?"

"Panic."

That made him smile. "Well, obviously."

"They come on when I start to feel over-whelmed, when there's too much going on in my head." She suddenly seemed wary. "Why do you want to know?"

"I'm just curious." She continued to look at him, her brows low over her bright blue eyes. "Why are you looking at me like that?"

"I've never told anyone about my panic attacks," she said, as if he'd somehow forced it out of her. "You now know my weakness."

"You say that as if you're not supposed to have any." He reached past her and started picking bark off the tree absently. "We all have weaknesses."

"Do you?"

"Oh, yes." She had no idea.

He continued picking at the tree until she put her hand on his and made him stop. "And you're not going to tell me?"

He took a deep breath. "It's complicated."

"I get it," she said, and turned to walk back to the shoreline. "You don't want to tell me."

He jogged after her. "No, it's not that I don't want to tell you. It's more like . . . I have to *show* you."

She stopped. He almost ran into her. "So show me."

"I can't. Not now." He ran his hands through his hair, frustrated. "You'll have to trust me on that."

"I don't have much of a choice, do I?" she said.

They headed around the lake, quiet again, and eventually circled back to the house. It was a long walk, and when they got back, Penny brought lunch out to them unasked. After she set out the plates of sandwiches and fruit, she passed behind Emily's chair, still in Win's view. She smiled as she pointed to Emily and gave him a thumbs-up before she went inside to answer the ringing phone.

He smiled back at her.

After they'd finished, Emily stood and walked to the railing. He followed the line of her long legs, up her body, to her face. He was suddenly fascinated by the progress of her hair tie as it slowly slipped out of her hair as she moved and stretched. Finally, the tie fell from the tips of her hair to the deck. She didn't seem to notice.

"I wish I had my bathing suit," she said. "I'd go cool off in the water."

"Come inside where it's cool. I'll show you around."

When she turned, he reached over to pick up her hair tie. "You dropped something."

She held out her hand. "Thanks."

But he put it in his pocket.

"You're not going to give it back?" she asked.

"Eventually," he said as he walked into the cavernous living room off the deck. Emily followed, arguing with him about rights of ownership.

She fell silent when she stepped inside. There weren't any paintings of sand dunes or antique wooden buoys on the walls, the way he knew some of the surrounding lake house rentals were decorated, like they could double as fish-house restaurants. This place actually looked like his family spent a lot of time here, which they did. The furniture was comfortable and had a bit of sag. One wall was dominated by a flat screen, and the floor under it was littered with a Wii and tons of DVDs. Overnight travel was inconvenient for them, so their vacations usually consisted of coming out to the lake and staying here.

"This is a lot more homey than I expected," she finally said.

"They can't all be ivory towers."

He led her to the second story with a cursory wave to the four bedrooms there, then up to the third-story loft, through a door in the linen closet. The space was occupied only by a low couch, a stack of books, a television, and some storage boxes. No one came up here but him. He loved his family, but when they were all out here, sometimes he needed a break from their *togetherness*. So this was where he went. He didn't like their house on Main Street as much—with its cold marble and oppressive history—but it was a lot easier to avoid people there.

"I spend a lot of time in this loft when I'm here," he said as she looked around. The only light was from the windows on the far wall, stacked in the shape of a triangle that followed the line of the sloping ceiling. Pink dust motes sparkled in the air.

"I can see why. It has a secret feel to it. It suits

you." She walked to the bank of windows. "Great view."

He watched her from across the room, backlit against the windows. He was moving before he was even aware of what he was doing. He stopped directly behind her, mere inches away. Awareness immediately radiated from her like electricity.

A full minute passed before he said, "You're suddenly quiet."

He watched her swallow. "I don't understand how you do this to me."

He leaned in slightly. Her hair smelled like something flowery, like the fading scent of lilacs. "Do what?"

"Your touch."

"I'm not touching you, Emily."

She turned around. "That's just it. It feels like you are. How do you do that? It's like you have something surrounding you, something I can't see, that reaches out. It doesn't make sense."

That startled him. She felt it. No one had ever felt it before.

She waited for him to say something, to explain or deny it, neither of which he could do. He took a step past her, closer to the window. "Your family once owned all of this," he said.

She hesitated before deciding to accept the change of subject. "All of what?"

"All of Piney Woods Lake. Years ago, that's how the Shelbys made their money, by selling it off, parcel by parcel." He pointed to the trees in the distance. "All that wooded acreage on the other side of the lake still belongs to your grandfather. That's millions of dollars of potential development. It drives my father crazy. He wants your grandfather to sell him some of it."

"Why?"

"Coffeys have always liked to have a say in the growth of Mullaby. Homesites, businesses, things like that."

"Why?" she asked again.

"Because this is our home. For years and years, we thought this was the only place we could live."

"Is it?"

He turned to face her. "Do you really want to know?" *My weakness.*

"Yes. Yes, of course I do."

This was it. There was no going back after he told her. He *had* to show her then. "The men in my family have an . . . affliction."

She looked confused. "What sort of affliction?"

He left her at the window and paced across the room. "It's genetic," he said. "A simple mutation. But it's particularly strong in my family. My grandfather had it. My uncle had it. My father has it." He paused. "I have it."

"Have what?"

He took a deep breath. "We call it The Glowing."

Emily stared at him, still not understanding.

"Our skin gives off light at night," he explained,

and it was amazing, actually saying that to someone outside his family. It was as liberating as he thought it would be. It was even better. The words were out and he couldn't take them back. He waited for Emily to say something. But she said nothing. "That's what you feel," he said eagerly, walking back to her and putting his hands on either side of her face, almost, but not quite, touching her.

She met his eyes. "You want me to believe that you glow in the dark," she said in a monotone.

Win dropped his hands. "You'll believe I'm a werewolf, but not this?"

"I never believed you were a werewolf."

He stepped back, trying not to feel defeated. He had to go on. "It goes back generations. My ancestors left the old country to avoid persecution, because people assumed their affliction was the work of evil. They traveled by sea, and history is riddled with sightings of their ship, said to be a portent of doom. When they came to America, Native Americans called them Spirits of the Moon. They settled here when it was nothing but farmland, far away from everyone, but slowly the town grew around them. No one knew their secret, and they realized they liked it, liked not being so isolated. But the stories of persecution were always handed down, scaring us into secrecy, even in the modern world. That all changed the night your mother tricked my uncle into coming out at night. He stood on the bandstand that summer night, in front of the entire town, and for the first time, everyone saw what we could do."

"That's a very elaborate story," she said.

"Emily, you've even seen me. In your backyard at night."

That gave her a start. "*You're* the light in my backyard? *You're* the Mullaby lights?"

"Yes."

He could tell her mind was working, trying to sort it all out. "Then why have you stopped coming around?"

"I come every night. But your grandfather sits on the kitchen porch below your balcony and tells me to go away before you can see that I'm there."

"My grandfather knows?" Her voice was pitching higher.

"Yes."

"Prove it." She looked around and saw the closet door. She walked over to it and opened it. There was nothing inside but a rain jacket and a single water ski. "Here, come here."

He walked over to her and she herded him into the closet and followed, closing the door behind them. It was a tight fit. She waited a few moments in the pitch black before she said, "Ha! I don't see you glowing."

"That's because it takes moonlight," he said patiently.

She snorted. "Well, that's convenient."

"Actually, no, it's not."

229

"This is ridiculous," she said, and he felt her fumbling to find the doorknob.

"Wait," he said, and reached out to stop her. His hand landed on her hip and she suddenly stilled. "Meet me tonight at the bandstand. At midnight. I'll show you."

"Why are you doing this?" she asked in a whisper. "Is this some elaborate plan?"

She caught him off guard with that. If she knew he was manipulating her, why was she letting him? "Plan?"

"For getting back at my mother for what she did."

"No," he said. "I told you before, I don't blame you for what she did."

"But you're re-creating that night with my mother and your uncle."

"It has nice symmetry, doesn't it?"

"Okay," she said unhappily. "I'll be there."

He almost laughed. "You don't have to sound so enthusiastic."

"This would be easier if I didn't like you so much."

"You like me?" He felt both elated and ashamed. She didn't answer. "How much?" he asked quietly, the air filling with tension.

"Enough to meet you tonight, even though I'm pretty sure you have something else planned other than glowing in the dark."

"That isn't enough?" He could sense her holding her breath when she realized how close his face was to hers. "I'm knotted up with you," he said. "Don't you feel it? From the moment we met. I was meant to show you."

"I need to go." She opened the door, and a blinding burst of light hit them. She was gone in seconds.

He caught up with her on the deck as she was putting on her shoes. "Don't go through the woods tonight. Come into the park from the street."

She stood and stared at him for a long time. He started to reach out his hand to touch her, to reassure her as much as himself, but she gave him a brief nod before turning and quickly making her way down the steps to the beach.

He watched her walk away, then he put his hands in his pockets and walked slowly, thoughtfully, back into the house.

He stopped when he entered the living room.

His father was sitting in the big black leather chair by the couch, his legs crossed.

Win was so astonished he couldn't speak for a moment. He could usually feel when his father was looking for him. Finally he said, "When did you get here?"

"Just now. I called earlier to ask you not to block your mother's car when you come home, because she's leaving early tomorrow with Kylie to go to Raleigh to shop for school clothes. Penny said you were on the beach. I asked with whom. She said a girl. I asked her to describe the girl, and it sounded like Emily Benedict. But I thought, No, Win knows better than that."

That must have been the phone call Penny had answered earlier. Win had to give her credit for doing what she could. She'd told his father he was on the beach with Emily, not that he was in the house alone with her. "So you came out to see for yourself," Win concluded. He took a deep breath and said, "I like her."

"I liked a girl once, when I was your age," Morgan said, steepling his fingers. "Her name was Veronica. She was new to Mullaby, too. All I wanted to do was spend all day staring at her. I asked her to a matinée, and your grandfather found out. He slapped me, then locked me in my room. When I didn't show up at the movie theater, Veronica came to the house to ask if I was all right. Your grandfather was horrible to her. He told her that my asking her out was just a joke. She hated me after that. But he made his point."

"What point?"

"That we weren't made for normal lives."

"Did your father treat your brother the same way?" Win asked as he took a seat on the couch.

"The rules weren't any different for Logan."

Win had never known that his grandfather hit his father. Win remembered the old man vaguely. He was very quiet when Win knew him. People used to say he was never the same after his youngest son, Logan, committed suicide. It made sense now that Logan and Dulcie Shelby had to sneak around. Win's grandfather obviously would have slapped Logan and locked him in his room if he'd found out. It all seemed so ridiculous now. The extreme measures. The furtive prowling. The secret was out and it couldn't be taken back.

"It's different now," Win said.

"You say that as if different is better," Morgan said. "If we wait long enough, people will forget what they saw, and things can go back to the way they were. It's just a matter of time. Sometimes I even hope your mother has forgotten."

"I don't want to go back to the way things were."

"You don't have a choice. You're grounded. And you're not allowed to associate with Emily anymore."

That wasn't unexpected. "That girl you liked. Didn't you ever want to tell her?"

Morgan uncrossed his legs, then crossed them again. He stared at his cuticles awhile. "No," he finally said. "I liked the illusion. When I was with her, I was . . ."

"Normal," Win finished for him.

Morgan nodded. "It was like that with your mother for a while. Then Logan was tricked into showing everyone what we could do. Your mother and I had only been married for two years. Nothing has been the same. She's never forgiven me for not telling her, for making her find out with the rest of the town."

Every Coffey man had a different way of telling the woman he married, but it was always after the ceremony. A tradition, like all the others, that made no sense. Win had often wondered, if Logan had never revealed the family secret, would his father have ever even told his mother?

"Mom loves you," Win said, certain that it had been true at least once.

Morgan got up and headed for the front door. "She loves me in the daytime. Everyone loves us in the daytime. Trust me on this, Win. I'm trying to save you some misery."

Chapter 14

*J*ulia parked her truck by the Dumpster behind the restaurant and thought, *What in the hell have I just done?* Sawyer had gotten her so mad that she'd slept with him. Or was that really the reason? Maybe it had just been the excuse she'd needed. But everything was messed up now. She didn't know what to do. There was no goal now, no plan. And now she had to go into her restaurant, which was already packed, wearing the same clothes she'd been wearing yesterday, and smelling of him. She adjusted the rearview mirror and looked at herself. God, she even had beard burn.

She groaned and put her head on the steering

wheel. She could go home, she supposed. But then people might come by and ask where she'd been, if something was wrong. It wasn't worth all the additional explaining. And Sunday was the busiest day at the restaurant, the day that brought in the most money. She had to do this.

She tried to smooth her hair back a little, but it didn't help much. She sighed and got out.

Coming in through the back meant walking a few steps into the seating area itself, just past the restrooms. She tried to sneak in, but found herself stopping when she saw just how full the place was. She knew how well the business was doing from a financial standpoint, but it was an entirely different experience to see it for herself. Her father would have *loved* this. He would have been out there talking to people, making them feel welcome, catching up on news. For a moment, she could even see him, in his T-shirt and jeans, ball cap and half-apron. He was a wisp of man, another ghost in her life. But then someone passed by her line of vision and she lost him. She suddenly wondered, when she left this place, would he still be here? Would his memory live on?

"Hey, Julia!" someone called from a table, and several people turned to her. More people called out. A few waved. A couple of old ladies she'd gone to church with when she was a kid even got up to invite her to the Sunday night service. Normally, she was here so early that she never saw these people. Oh, she would see them in the grocery store and on the street, but they were never this friendly. For some reason, seeing her here made it different for them. Here, she was the restaurant owner. She was the reason they still had this place to come to, to gather, to socialize. Here, she was Jim's daughter. And they saw in that something to be admired.

Julia smiled at them, a little dazed, and side-stepped her way into the kitchen.

Hours later, in the thick of the lunch rush, Julia finally finished her cakes. They were being sliced and served even as she stood behind the counter and wrote the names of the day's cakes on the chalkboard.

She didn't know it, but while she was in the kitchen, her stepmother, Beverly, had come in, but obviously not to eat. She was waiting for Julia at a table near the door. When she got up, the couple she'd been sitting with looked relieved.

"Julia!" Beverly said as she approached, waving a large brown envelope. Several men looked her way. "I stopped by Stella Ferris's house looking for you because you're never here at the restaurant at lunchtime. What *are* you doing here at lunchtime? You're only here early in the morning. Everyone knows that. You should set a routine and stick to it."

Julia was too tired, both emotionally and physically, to deal with Beverly today. She set the chalkboard down. "Let's talk some other time, Beverly. I'm exhausted and I want to go home." And where was that, exactly? she thought. Her apartment at Stella's? Her dad's old house? Baltimore? Nothing was clear anymore.

"No, no, no. I'm put out enough with you already, missy. If I had known you'd be here, I would have come here first instead of stopping at Stella's house and waiting for you. That woman is such an odd duck. What *are* you doing here at lunchtime?" she asked again. "You're never here at lunchtime."

"I own this place, Beverly. I can come and go anytime I please."

"Speaking of which . . . Excuse me, hon," she said to a man sitting at the counter as she hipped her way between him and the man beside him. It was a tight fit, but she didn't seem to mind. Neither did the men. "Here's the surprise I was talking about!" She slapped the envelope on the counter in front of Julia. "Your father would be so proud of me. I had my lawyer draw up partnership papers for this place. All you have to do is sign over half of J's Barbecue to me. That way, when we sell it, we can split the profit."

The men on either side of Beverly looked at Julia curiously, waiting, as Beverly was, for her to say something. People at a nearby table heard, too. The news soon made its way around the room like smoke.

Julia stared at the envelope on the counter. This shouldn't have mattered, but it did. Just like last night shouldn't have mattered, but it did.

At least a full minute passed before Beverly began to look uncomfortable. "Now, Julia, you know I deserve this." She leaned in and said in a softer voice, "I thought we had an understanding."

"My understanding," Julia said, finally looking up from the envelope, "is that my father loved you, but you left him."

That had the restaurant quiet in seconds.

Beverly scooped up the envelope. "Obviously, you're cranky. From the look of you, you haven't had much sleep. And don't think I haven't noticed that those are the same clothes you were wearing yesterday. Clean up a little, and I'll meet you outside."

"No, Beverly. This ends here," Julia said, and it all came flooding out. "You were everything to him, to the detriment of his relationship with me. I ceased to exist when you came into his life. These scars you like to point out every time you see me were because he wouldn't look at me once you appeared. He worked damn hard at this business, but it was never good enough for you, was it? When it stopped making money, as paltry as it had been, you left him. Do you honestly think I'm going to give you half of it? That you *deserve* it?"

Beverly pursed her thin lips, which were lined in pearly peach. "You could learn a thing or two about casting stones. *You* left him first. And you were the reason he was so deeply in debt. It was all *your* fault, missy, so don't get all high and mighty on me."

Julia couldn't believe her gall. "How could I be the reason he was in debt?"

Beverly laughed resentfully. "How do you think he paid for that reformatory you went to? What little he made was still too much to apply for aid, and because you were from out of state, the fee was even higher. He mortgaged everything he had for you, you ungrateful girl. And I *still* didn't leave him then. I only left when Bud started showing an interest in me and your father didn't say a word about it. He stopped appreciating me a long time ago. All he talked about was *you*. How *you* were the first in his family to go to college, how *you* lived in the big city, how *you* were making your dream come true. He conveniently forgot that you tried to shred yourself to pieces, that you got knocked up at sixteen, that you took all his money and then never came back to see him."

Julia could see the surprise on the faces of some people in the restaurant. What people didn't know about the scars on her arms, they inferred, but no one knew she'd been pregnant when she left.

As blindsided as she was by this news, by what her father had sacrificed for her, something in her mind clicked, and it made perfect sense. He'd never been good at expressing himself. She'd spent a long time in therapy, trying to adjust her expectations, especially from the men in her life. She'd thought she'd wanted grand gestures and expressive declarations, because her father never gave her that. Sometimes she thought that even falling for Sawyer when she was a teenager, how larger-than-life he was, was looking for something missing in her relationship with her father. But how could she have missed this? Everything her father did was quiet. Even loving her. The tragedy was that no one in her father's life had ever understood that. Everyone had left him because they'd hadn't been quiet enough to hear him. Not until it was too late.

But no, she thought. It wasn't too late.

Tears came to Julia's eyes. She wiped them away. She couldn't believe she was doing this in front of everyone. "He was a good, uncomplicated man," Julia said. "And he deserved better than us both. You're not going to get any piece of this restaurant, Beverly. No one is. This was the one thing that never let him down. His only constant. Too many people have taken too many things from him as it is." She pointed to the door. "You're not welcome here ever again."

"Oh, I'll be back," Beverly said, sashaying to the door. "When you leave, I'll be right back in here and there won't be a thing you can do about it."

"I'll be sure she knows she's not welcome," Charlotte, the day manager, said from behind Julia.

"So will I," the new waitress said.

"I'll remind her," one of the men at the counter said.

"Me too," said someone across the room. The restaurant then became a chorus of agreement.

Beverly looked aghast. She glared at Julia. "See, this is what you do! You go and leave all sorts of trouble behind."

"I've got news for you," Julia said. *"I'm not leaving."*

The restaurant erupted into applause as Beverly left.

Julia stood there, breathing heavily, and thought again, *What in the hell have I just done?*

"**THERE YOU** are!" Stella said, meeting her at the door when Julia finally got home. She was wearing what she called her day gown, a silk robe with buttons her mother had given her. She said it made her feel like a lady of leisure. "I've been so worried! Where were you last night? Even your evil stepmother came by looking for you."

"Why did you sleep with Sawyer?" Julia blurted out, right there in the foyer. She hadn't meant to say it. She was as surprised as Stella looked.

"What?" Stella said.

"Sawyer said you slept together, three years ago. Do you love him?"

"Oh, that," Stella said. "It was terrible. Not the sex . . . at least what I remember of it. But I was a mess. My divorce had just been finalized and all my money was gone. Sawyer came by that evening to give me a bottle of champagne to celebrate my freedom. I got drunk and I climbed all over him. I'm not proud of it. Believe me, I never wanted to be the woman men had sex with out of pity. It was just once, and I tried to avoid him after that, but he wouldn't let me. Sawyer's a good guy. A good friend. Why do you ask?" Stella clutched at her heart dramatically. "Oh my God! That's where you were last night! You totally did it with Sawyer!"

Julia didn't answer, but she must have given something away with her look.

Stella drew her into her arms for a tight hug. "I'm so happy. That man has always had a thing for you. I have no idea why he waited so long. I used to tease him that he was afraid of you." She took Julia's hand and led her to the living room, where she had been fortifying herself with a pitcher of Bloody Marys. "So, tell me everything! What happened? When? How many times?"

Julia shook her head as she sat down and accepted the drink Stella gave her. "Uh-uh. No way."

"You have to tell me. You're my best friend," Stella said, which startled Julia. "It's the code. I tell you everything that's happening in *my* life."

"You didn't tell me about Sawyer," she said, taking the celery stalk out of the drink and biting into it.

"Sawyer isn't happening in my life. He already happened. A long time ago."

Julia set the glass back on the tray. "Am I really your best friend?"

"Of course you are."

"But you used to laugh at me in high school."

Surprised, Stella sat down heavily on the chair opposite Julia. "High school was a long time ago. Are you saying you can't be my best friend now because of what happened back then?"

"No," Julia said, being honest with herself for the first time in a long time. Her friendships in Baltimore had never felt like this. Her friends there had accepted her for who they thought she was. Stella accepted her for who she *really* was. This place defined her. It always had. Stella knew that. "I think you're the best friend I've ever had."

"That's more like it," Stella said. "Now, tell me *everything*."

THE FIRST thing Sawyer said when Julia opened the door a few hours later was, "Let's get this out of the way. There's nothing going on between me and Holly."

Julia leaned against the doorjamb. It was so nice to see him, but there was so much that needed to be said. "The two of you look good together. You match. Have you ever considered getting back together?"

"I don't want to match. Holly is selling me her part of the house we own together here. She's getting remarried in a couple of weeks. She's pregnant. I completely forgot that she was coming to town this weekend."

"That was my fault. Sorry."

"Don't be sorry. Do it again." He tried to step into her apartment, but she froze, her hand on the doorknob. He stepped back. "You don't want me to come in?"

"No, it's not that. It's just . . . I've always treated this place as temporary. There's not much to it." After all this time, she couldn't believe she was still embarrassed.

"I don't care what your apartment looks like."

"Automatic response. Sorry." She opened the door wider.

He stepped inside with a deep breath and a satisfied smile. He put his hands on his hips and looked like he'd conquered the New World. "I've wanted up here ever since you've been back. And it's not what you're thinking. On Thursdays when I have pizza with Stella, that incredible smell from whatever you happen to be baking . . . it never fails to make me heady."

"Could you see it?" Julia asked.

"I can always see it. It's on you now, sparkling in your hair." He pointed to her hand. "You have some in the cuff of your sleeve, too."

Julia turned the cuff inside out and, sure enough,

flour and sugar from that morning sprinkled out. "That's amazing."

"Are you going to give me a tour?" Sawyer asked.

"We can do it from here." She pointed to each door. "Bedroom, bathroom, kitchen, living room." She led him to the tiny living room and invited him to take a seat. She remained standing, too nervous to sit. "Stella's mother gave me that love seat. I have a nice couch of my own in storage up in Baltimore."

"Do you think you'll bring it down?"

"I don't know."

He sat back, obviously making a concerted effort not to push the subject. "Did you actually get into a fight with Beverly at your restaurant this morning?"

That made Julia suddenly laugh. "Did Stella tell you, or did word travel that fast?"

"Both. What happened?"

"I had a few things to get off my chest. So did she, apparently."

"I heard that you said you weren't selling the restaurant," he said carefully.

"What can I say? I'm as surprised as you are."

"What about your two-year plan?" He hesitated. "Does this mean you're staying?"

She didn't answer right away. "You know that big thing I wanted to tell you? I'm going to tell you now. Then I'm going to leave you alone to let you think about it, okay?"

A guarded look came to his face. "Alone, as in leaving and never coming back?"

"Alone, as in leaving this apartment for a walk," she said. "Then, who knows?"

"Okay," he said. "Lay it on me."

"Stay right there." She went to her bedroom and reached under her bed, feeling around until she found the old algebra textbook she had hidden there. She opened the book and looked at the two photos she had of her baby. Sawyer's baby. She'd put the photos in this book when she was at Collier, and could never think of anywhere else to store them. She set the book on her bed and took the photos to the living room. She felt jumpy, and her skin was alive with a thousand prickles.

He looked up at her as she entered. Before she could talk herself out of it, she held the photos out to him and he took them.

She watched as he looked at them, confused at first, then alert. He met her eyes with a short, quick jerk of his head.

"She was born on May fifth," she said. "Six pounds, six ounces. She looked nothing like me and everything like you. Blond hair and blue eyes. A couple from Washington, D.C., adopted her."

"I have a daughter?"

She nodded, then left before he could ask any more questions.

HEAT RADIATED from the metal bleachers in blurry, undulating light. Julia's spot when she was a teenager was where the top bleacher butted against the enclosed media box, forming a pocket of concrete shade.

She hadn't been here since she was sixteen. It felt different, but eerily the same. From here, she could see down onto the fifty-yard line where it had all happened, where her life had changed. The lumbering brick school building on the far side of the field was quiet, but the windows were open, indicating that teachers were in their classrooms, getting ready for the new school year. The cafeteria was on the ground floor and faced the field. She thought of what Sawyer had said about how he used to watch her on the bleachers at lunch.

She'd been there for at least an hour, wondering how much time he needed with this, or if all the time in the world wouldn't be enough, when something suddenly caught her eye and, on the left side of the field, she saw Sawyer walking toward her.

He stopped at the base of the bleachers and looked up at her. The photos were in his hand. It was hard to tell his expression. Was he mad? Would this change everything all over again? The protective part of her steeled herself for that possibility, even though she knew she wasn't as easily hurt as she'd been when she was sixteen. She had a lot fewer expectations than she did then. She had a very long list of Things She Would Never Have, and Sawyer had always been on that list, along with her daughter, long fingers, and the ability to turn back time.

He started up the bleachers toward her. The first step he took, he was sixteen, blond and cherubic, the wish every girl in school made when she blew out candles on her birthday cake. With every step he took, he got older, the cherubic cheeks giving way to sharper cheekbones, his skin growing more golden, his hair a darker blond. By the time he reached her, he was the Sawyer of today, of this morning . . . of last night.

Without a word, he sat beside her.

"How did you know I would be here?" she asked, because even she didn't know she'd be here until she'd walked by and saw the school.

"Just a hunch."

"Go ahead," she said. "Ask."

"I don't have to ask the big question. I know why you didn't tell me."

She nodded. "Okay."

"Do you know where she is now? What she's doing?" He looked at the photos. "Her name?"

"No." She tugged on the cuffs of her sleeves. "The papers are sealed. I can't find her unless she wants to find me. You said you followed the scent home when your mother baked, so I have it in my head—in my heart—that if I just keep baking, she'll find me. That this will bring her home." Julia looked down, then across the field. Anywhere but him. "I think she has your sweet sense. I couldn't eat enough cake to satisfy her when I was pregnant."

248

"That's what my mother said when she was pregnant with me."

"I wanted to keep her so badly," she said. "For a long time, I was angry at everyone for not helping me make that happen. It took a while to realize that it was just misplaced guilt, because I wasn't well enough to care for her on my own."

He was the one to look away this time. "Saying I'm sorry doesn't feel like enough. I feel like I owe you so much more. I owe you for her." He shook his head. "I can't believe I have a daughter."

"You don't owe me anything," she said. "She was a gift."

"Your hair is still pink in this photo." He lifted the one of her holding the baby in the hospital. "When did you stop dyeing it?"

"When I went up to school. I cut it all off shortly after that photo was taken."

"When did you start with the pink streak?"

Julia nervously tucked it behind her ear. "In college. My friends in Baltimore think I do it to be edgy. But I do it because it reminds me of what I can get through . . . of what I *have* gotten through. It reminds me not to give up."

There was a long silence. A maintenance man on a riding lawn mower drove onto the football field and started taking wide loops around it. Julia and Sawyer watched him. "Are you going to stay?" Sawyer finally asked.

How did she answer that? He was being very

calm. She had no idea how he really felt. "I spent so much time telling myself that this wasn't home that I started to believe it," she said carefully. "Belonging has always been tough for me."

"I can be your home," he said quietly. "Belong to me."

She stared at him, stunned by his whispered grand gesture, until he turned to her. When he saw the tears in her eyes, he reached for her. She held on to him and cried, cried for so long her throat ached, cried until the football field was all mown and the air smelled of cut grass, and bugs swarmed the track.

To think, after all this time, after all the searching and all the waiting, after all the regret and the time she'd spent away, she came back to find that happiness was right where she'd left it.

On a football field in Mullaby, North Carolina.

Waiting for her.

Chapter 15

Emily stuffed her hands in her shorts pockets as she walked down the sidewalk that night. There were no cars out, but she kept listening for them, stepping into the darkness in between each streetlight and pausing, waiting for some indication that Win had invited the whole town to this, like her mother had done.

Since coming to Mullaby, Emily had discovered

that her disbelief could be suspended further than she ever thought it could, and there was a small part of her that wondered, what if it was true? If giants exist, if wallpaper can change on its own . . . why couldn't Win do . . . what he said he could do? If it was real, that meant this wasn't about revenge. This wasn't about what her mother had done. The closer she got the more she *wanted* it to be true.

When she reached Main Street, she stopped on the sidewalk by the park. No one was there. Gray-green moonlight illuminated the area, and the shadows from the trees in the back looked like brittle witches' fingers reaching across the grass toward her. She took a step into the park, then made herself walk to the bandstand.

She stood a few feet away from the main staircase and stared up at it, all the way up to the crescent moon weathervane, then she turned back to the street, to see if Win was coming from that direction.

"You came. I didn't think you would."

His voice startled her, coming out of nowhere. "Where are you?" she called into the park, her eyes darting around, the shadows playing tricks on her.

"Behind you." She spun back to the bandstand. Her hands had started shaking, so she curled them into fists, her fingernails biting into her palms. Looking closely, she could finally make out a figure in a dark pool at the back of the stage.

She felt her heart sink.

"You're not glowing." she said, and it was an accusation, like he'd forgotten her birthday or stepped on her toe and didn't say he was sorry. It hurt, and she felt stupid for letting it. There wasn't anything supernatural to this. It was simple, and simple was good. Easier to understand. That was why she'd shown up tonight, after all. To let him play his trick on her. To try to right some wrongs.

She saw him rise, his white suit standing out against the shadows. He walked to the steps and slowly descended. He stopped on the grass, a few feet away from her. She met his eyes defiantly. *Give it to me,* she thought. *I can take it.*

It took a moment for her to realize that Win looked nervous, unsure. That's when it happened. Like blowing on embers, a light began to grow around him. It looked like he was backlit, but of course there was no light source around him. It was as if radiant heat was emanating from his skin, surrounding him in waving white light. He looked like a dream of daylight in the middle of night. His light was almost alive, undulating, reaching out. It was utterly, terrifyingly beautiful.

He stood there and let her stare at him. His shoulders seemed to relax a little when he realized she wasn't going to run away. But it wasn't because she didn't want to. She simply couldn't. Her muscles felt frozen.

He took one step toward her, then another. She

could see the light as it began to stretch toward her. Then she felt it, those ribbons of warmth. It was usually comforting, that feeling, but it was a decidedly different experience to actually *see* what was happening.

"Stop," she said, her voice thin and breathless. She was finally able to take a few steps backward by leaning back, as if to fall, and her legs instinctively moved to keep her upright. "Just stop."

He stopped immediately as she stumbled away. "Are you all right?" he asked.

Was she all right? No, she wasn't all right! She turned her back on him and put her hands on her knees. She couldn't get enough air.

"There's nothing to be afraid of, Emily."

"How are you doing that?" she demanded. "Make it stop!"

"I can't. But I can get out of the moonlight. Come over to the steps. Sit down."

"Don't," she said, looking over her shoulder and seeing that he was making another move toward her. "Just do what you have to do to make it go away."

He took the steps two at a time and retreated into the shadows of the stage. She gratefully tripped to the steps to sit. She put her head down and tried to concentrate on something random. *The word* lethologica *describes the state of not being able to remember the word you want.*

She eventually lifted her head as the spots faded

from her eyes. She felt chilled from her cold sweat.

"I didn't mean to make you panic," Win said from behind her. "I'm sorry."

It helped not having to turn around to look at him yet. "Are there people here watching? Are we being filmed? Is that what this is all about?"

"This isn't a trick," he said, an ocean of heartache in those words. "It's who I am."

She took a deep breath and wiped her forehead with the back of her hand. If this was real . . . then she understood why the town was so shocked when her mother brought Win's uncle out at night.

Strange and wondrous things, indeed.

"How do you feel?" he asked. "Can I get you something?"

"No, just stay there." She finally stood and faced the bandstand again. "Everyone here knows?"

"Everyone who was there that night," he said from the darkness. "My family made sure no one has seen it since."

"But they know that you're the light in the woods?"

"Yes. I've been doing it since I was a kid, but plenty of my ancestors did it before me."

"Why did you want me to see it?"

He hesitated, as if he wasn't entirely sure now. She suddenly felt horrible, like she'd let him down. Her mother had raised her better than this. She'd raised her to accept and respect, to help and to never be afraid to get involved. All her life had been leading up to this, and she'd failed. She'd failed Win. She'd failed her mother.

She was still in the history loop. She was scared now, scared for herself, scared for Win, knowing how this had turned out last time.

"I've never known how to step up to people and say, 'This is me. Accept me for who I am,' " Win finally said. "I knew from the moment I met you, I was meant to show you. I thought you were meant to help."

"How?" she asked immediately. "How can I help you? I don't understand."

"You can tell me that, now that you've seen this, your feelings are no different than they are in the daytime. That's all."

She squared her shoulders and backed farther into the open park. "Come down here, Win."

"Are you sure?"

"Yes."

He walked back down and his skin started burning again. He looked ready to bolt back up the steps if necessary. She held her ground, even though her stomach was leaping.

When he finally made it to her, she reached out and took his hand in hers right away, to steady herself as much as him. She was surprised that his hand was simply warm, as warm as it always was, not scorching hot. "Does it hurt?" she asked.

"No."

She swallowed. She was trembling. Could he

feel it? "I think it's beautiful. I think it's the most beautiful thing I've ever seen."

He stood there, glowing like the sun, and stared at her like she was the unbelievable one. He angled closer to her, and the closer he came, the more the glowing seemed to stretch out to her. It felt like walking into sunshine from the shade. His light surrounded them both, jumping around as if saying, *Together, together, now!* She saw him tilt his head slightly.

He's going to kiss me, she suddenly thought. She knew it in a way she couldn't explain. Like how you know a certain day is going to be good the moment you wake up. She'd thought about this a lot, more than she cared to admit, but somehow she'd never imagined it quite like this. It was nothing like she'd expected. And yet . . . it was strangely perfect.

But before it could happen, they jerked away from each other, startled, when they heard quick footsteps. Win's sister was running across the park toward them.

"Win! What are you doing?" Kylie said breathlessly, skidding to a stop on the dewy grass. "Dad wants you to come back inside. Right *now*."

Emily and Win exchanged glances. She wasn't used to seeing him this unsure. "What happens now?" Emily asked.

"Now we deal with the consequences and move on. Just like last time, only—"

"Better," she finished for him.

He touched her cheek and smiled, then ran across the park toward his house. Emily and Kylie watched him go. What a ravishing sight he was.

"It's beautiful, isn't it?" Kylie said.

Emily turned to her warily, surprised she was being so nice to her now. "Yes," she said softly.

"I would love to do what he does. He has no idea." Kylie paused. "All my life, I've heard stories of that night with my uncle and your mother. I thought you'd be like her. I'm glad you're not." She smiled, like she'd just given a compliment. Emily took it in the spirit it was intended, but would never get used to how the town thought of her mother, even now. The broken circle of history should have let all the animosity pour out. But it didn't. Emily might fit in here now. Her mother never would, though. "I better go see what's going on in there. I'll see you around. With Win, no doubt."

With no light to her skin, Kylie soon faded into the night. Emily stood there for a while before finally walking home.

EMILY WOKE to the sound of someone pounding on the front door. She sat up quickly. She'd been too stunned, too exhausted, to turn on her MP3 player before she'd gone to bed. When she looked around, the new phases-of-the-moon wallpaper took her aback for a moment. That's when it all came rushing back to her, everything she'd seen last night.

He glowed.

Then, out of nowhere, the thought: *He almost kissed me.*

The pounding continued and Emily climbed out of bed. She'd slept in her clothes, so she immediately jogged to her bedroom door and down the stairs.

To her surprise, the first thing she noticed was that the front door was closed. Vance usually left it open when he went to breakfast. She'd just reached the bottom stair when the accordion door to Vance's room swung open. Grandpa Vance walked out, comb marks still in his wet hair. He hadn't left for breakfast yet. How early was it?

Vance didn't notice her on the staircase as he walked to the front door and unlocked it.

"We need to talk," Morgan Coffey said from the porch. His white linen suit was rumpled, like he'd been wearing it all night. His dark hair, normally gelled, was falling across his forehead. It made him look younger, more like Win.

"Morgan?" Vance said, obviously surprised. "What are you doing here at this hour?"

"Believe me, I would have been here earlier, but I had to wait until light."

"Come in." Vance stepped back and Morgan entered the foyer. "What's wrong?"

Morgan noticed Emily right away and stiffened.

His hatred rushed at her in one great wave. She actually took a step back up the staircase. "I take it your granddaughter hasn't told you yet," he said, nudging his chin at her. His stare was so hard that Vance put himself between them, as if protecting her. "Why did you let her come here in the first place, Vance? Hasn't your family done enough to hurt mine?"

"What happened?" Vance demanded.

"*It* happened," Morgan said. "Your granddaughter lured my son into the park last night. Just like last time."

"Emily had nothing to do with it," Win said from the porch. He opened the screen door and stepped inside. "I asked her to meet me there. And it was nothing like last time. Emily and I were the only two in the park."

"I told you to stay at home," Morgan said.

"This has to do with me. I am going to be here for it."

Grandpa Vance looked confused. He turned to her. "Emily?"

"I thought I would show up and he would do something to humiliate me, to get back at my mom for what she did. I didn't believe him when he said he glowed. I didn't believe him when he said to meet him and he'd show me."

"Child, why did you go if you thought he was going to humiliate you?" Vance asked incredulously.

"I thought it would help make up for—"

Vance held up one skillet-sized hand. "Stop, stop right there. You don't have to make up for anything your mother did. Morgan, this ends now."

"You're letting her off the hook, just like you did your daughter."

Grandpa Vance's face tightened. He was angry. And an angry giant was a sight to behold. "I never made excuses for Dulcie, and I have always accepted blame for what happened, for not being able to control her. But listen to me well, my granddaughter is *not* Dulcie and I will not have her treated this way."

Morgan cleared his throat. "I'd feel more comfortable if you sat down, Vance."

Vance didn't give an inch. "No one is ever comfortable around me. You, of all people, should know how that feels."

"I want her to stay away from my son."

"I've been watching your son in the woods behind my house for a while now. Emily staying away from him isn't the problem," Vance said pointedly.

Morgan shot an angry look at Win.

"You can't make me stay away from her," Win said.

"Did you learn nothing from your uncle?" Morgan asked him.

"Yes, I did. I learned from him that it takes courage to love someone your family doesn't approve of."

"You don't seriously love this girl," Morgan said with clear disbelief.

Emily couldn't take her eyes off him. He loved her? But Win simply stared at his father, a power struggle going on.

"My brother committed suicide because of her family," Morgan told Win. "Doesn't that mean anything to you?"

"It was his decision," Win said, and she was amazed by how composed he was. Morgan Coffey was a force to be reckoned with, but so was Win. She wondered if Morgan knew that, if he understood. So much that was incredible about Win seemed to be because of his father. "But I think ignoring what he sacrificed is stupid. He gave us an opportunity to live normal lives here."

"*My* life has not been normal since it happened! Your mother has never forgiven me for not telling her."

"And you want the same for me? I wanted to show her. I didn't want it to be a secret. And the world didn't end. She didn't reject me, Dad. This isn't you and Mom. This isn't Dulcie and Logan. This is me and Emily. It's an entirely different story."

In the silence that followed, Vance said, "Let them live their lives without our baggage, Morgan."

But Morgan wasn't going to let it go. He pointed to Emily. "Your daughter lured my brother into that park that night! She tricked him! She ruined everything."

"Lower your hand, Morgan," Vance said. "I'll say this only once more. My granddaughter is not Dulcie, and I will not tolerate you blaming her for her mother's sins."

"And what are you going to do about it?"

Vance took a single step toward him. "I'm going to tell the truth. You've made Logan and your family out to be the victims, and I let it happen because Dulcie wanted it that way. She left knowing she would be vilified. She left to make things easier on you, which was the first selfless thing she'd ever done."

Emily, who had been staring at Win all this time, suddenly turned her head sharply. "What are you talking about, Grandpa Vance?"

"Let's go, Win," Morgan said quickly.

"No, I want to hear this."

"Logan was troubled long before Dulcie came into his life," Vance said. "He'd tried to commit suicide several times, something no one but his family knew. But Logan told Dulcie. He and your mother were in love. At least, your mother was in love with him. I'd never seen her like that before. All over town, she carved their initials onto every wooden surface she could find."

"Wait, Mom carved those initials?" Emily asked. "Not Logan?"

He nodded. "She was smitten. She was usually

such a forceful girl, always getting her way, but she was very deferential to Logan. He was very shy in public, but he could control her like no one else in private. Knowing how angry it would make her, he told Dulcie that they couldn't be together because his family didn't approve of her. He said his family had too many secrets and wouldn't let him marry just anyone. But there was a solution, he told her. So Dulcie went along with inviting everyone in town to a so-called performance by her, aware that it was a ruse, an opportunity for Logan to come out at night in front of the whole town. But she thought it was simply going to be his symbolic declaration of love for her. Dulcie had no idea that the reason the Coffeys didn't come out at night was because they glowed. She thought, as we all did, it was just one more thing they did to keep themselves elite, to keep themselves separate from the middle-class masses in town. In fact, I can still remember when several of the more important families in town wouldn't come out at night just because the Coffeys didn't."

"She didn't trick him?" Emily asked.

"If anything, he tricked her. Dulcie was as stunned as the rest of us. Logan reached out to her after it happened, but she didn't want to talk to him. I don't know if it was his plan all along to commit suicide after he exposed his family's secret, or if he was just overcome with remorse afterward, possibly fueled by Dulcie's rejection.

Only his family knows that. I do know he *wanted* to reveal himself. He wanted people to know."

Emily couldn't help but think of the parallel to Win. His family had obviously been trying for acceptance for who they really were for generations.

Morgan's face had raspberry-red splotches on it now. "No one is going to believe you. They'll never believe Dulcie was an innocent party. And I will always maintain that she could have stopped him. She could have stopped him from stepping out onto that bandstand. She could have stopped him from killing himself. He *did* love her. He gave her that family heirloom." He pointed to Emily's wrist, to the charm bracelet. Emily automatically put her hand over it. "Our mother gave it to him to give to the woman he married, like it had been given to her on her wedding night. That he gave it to Dulcie had to mean something. But if he had fallen for someone less selfish, and more sympathetic, he might be alive today. Our secret might still be a secret. The way it was always meant to be."

"Emily knows the truth now," Grandpa Vance said calmly. "That's all that matters. I have no intention of telling anyone else."

She didn't know why it was so important for Morgan to have people believe his brother was tricked. Maybe it made dealing with the death of his brother easier. Or maybe it helped his family, knowing the town didn't think Logan was troubled or manipulative. It could only help, she thought, that there wasn't a stigma like that attached to their glowing. It probably made it easier for the town to accept what they'd seen, to sympathize. Emily realized that her mother had known this. That's why she'd taken the blame. And it had been her first step into the life of someone different. "I won't tell anyone, either," she said.

Morgan turned to Win. "I'll think about it," Win said.

"You'll think about it at home. You're grounded."

Morgan turned and walked to the front door. He held the screen door open for Win. But Win walked over to Vance. "I'd like to take your granddaughter on a date when my punishment is over, if I have your permission." Win held out his hand.

"Win!" Morgan said.

Vance seemed as surprised as Morgan, but he slowly held out his hand and shook Win's.

"Win! Now!"

Win turned, but not before he looked up at Emily, who was still on the staircase, and said, "I'll see you soon?"

She nodded. He gave her a reassuring smile, then turned and left.

Morgan let the screen slap shut loudly behind them.

Emily and Vance didn't move for a few

moments, both of them staring at the door. Emily finally turned to her grandfather. "Why didn't you tell me the truth from the beginning?"

"She made me swear not to tell anyone." He looked tired. He walked to the staircase and sat on the stairs, sinking like an anchor. She was still standing, but he was so large that he was taller than she was, even when he sat. "Lily had a cousin who lived in San Diego. I arranged for Dulcie to live with her. To go to school there. I gave her a large chunk of cash, and she left the day before Logan's funeral. She tried to make it work, but I don't think she knew where she fit in after what happened. She quit school after a few months. A few months later she ran away. I got postcards for a couple of years. Then nothing."

"Why didn't you look for her?" Emily said.

He shrugged. "Because I knew she didn't want to be found. She knew that if she contacted me, I would give her anything. But she didn't want that anymore. A good, decent life for her was only possible if she left everything behind. The Coffeys, Mullaby . . . me."

"She could have come back and told the truth!" Emily said. "And then everyone would have seen what a good person she became. She could have been redeemed."

"I think she found redemption in other ways," Grandpa Vance said, looking down at his clasped hands. "When she left, she told me that when she had children, she would never raise them the way I raised her. She said she would teach them responsibility. She said her children would be nothing like her. I like to think that at some point in her life she forgave me. But I deserve it if she didn't." He took a deep breath. "One thing is for sure, she did raise a remarkable daughter."

Emily paused, then sat beside him on the steps. She put her hand on his. "So did you, Grandpa Vance," she said.

And for the very first time, she thought maybe it was okay that they were the only two people here who knew that.

The point was, they knew.

VANCE DEBATED whether or not to go to breakfast that morning, but ultimately decided to go because he didn't want to answer questions about his absence. No one had to know what had occurred that morning.

When he came in from breakfast a few hours later, he was exhausted, and not his normal exhaustion, the kind he felt minute by minute. The tension from the confrontation with Morgan had manifested itself into a feeling of having survived a collision. His neck muscles ached and his joints were stiff. He was more than ready to lie down and take a nap.

But instead of going straight to his room, he went to check the dryer.

He hadn't meant to get so angry at Morgan. He didn't often get angry at other people. There was no sense in it. The person you were angry at was rarely ever repentant. Now, getting angry with *yourself* had some merit. It showed you had sense enough to chastise the one person who had any hope of benefiting from it. And he was plenty angry with himself.

For many, many things.

For letting this go too far. For living too much in the past. For not being a better parent to Dulcie. For missing so much of Emily's life already.

He walked to the laundry room and opened the dryer. He reached down, bending at the hip, and tried not to groan at the effort. He felt like such a small man, carrying around a body that was too big for him.

He reached in and expected to feel the smooth, cool curve of the dryer drum. Instead, his fingers brushed something slimy. Something that moved.

He jerked his hand away and stumbled back.

Out jumped a large frog.

He stared at it, frozen.

He watched it hop to the laundry room door, and for a moment he expected to see Lily's shoes. His eyes actually traveled up, hoping she would appear, standing there, laughing, like she had last time.

But no one was there.

He looked back down and saw that the frog was

gone. He quickly stepped out of the room, and when he crossed through the doorway, he felt like he'd walked through a fragrant breeze. His hair even moved. The sleeves of his shirt billowed.

He closed his eyes and took a deep breath.

Lily.

The air was sprinkled with her spirit. He stood still for a long time, not wanting to lose her. He took deep breaths, his heart aching as, with each breath, the scent faded.

And she was gone again.

When he opened his eyes, he saw the frog sitting at the kitchen door. It turned and wiggled through a tear in the screen. Vance automatically followed.

He opened the screen door to see the frog hop across the backyard. He walked after it, all the way to the back of the property. The frog stopped at the gazebo and stared at him.

Vance hesitated, then looked around. Emily had obviously been back here, trimming the boxwoods around the gazebo. He suddenly remembered that Dulcie had done that, too, after Lily had died. She'd tried so hard to keep things going on her own, and she'd only been twelve. He should have been there for her, he should have taken care of things, instead of throwing money at her. But he'd fallen apart, and everything around him had followed suit.

Lily wouldn't have wanted things like this. Maybe that's what she was trying to tell him. The last time she'd put a frog in the dryer was to tell him to stop dwelling on the way things used to be, to stop being afraid of change, of what came next.

He had to stop squandering what time he had left. He had a granddaughter to take care of.

He took a deep breath and nodded to the frog in agreement to a silent question. Okay. He would call his old gardener. He knew landscaping was still in that family. He'd get this place fixed up. He turned to look at the house. It looked nothing like when Lily was alive. He'd hire a roofer. A housepainter.

Yes.

And he'd give Emily an allowance. He'd have a talk with her about college. Maybe she would go to State, where Lily had gone, which was only a short drive away. Maybe she would want to come home on breaks. Maybe she would want to live here after she graduated.

Yes.

He would build her a house on the lake, as a wedding gift, maybe.

What if she married Win Coffey?

It wouldn't be a nighttime wedding, that was for sure.

Or, knowing Win, maybe it would be.

He smiled when he thought about how Emily would look on her wedding day. Lily's wedding dress was in the attic. Maybe she'd want to wear it.

Julia, of course, would make the cake.

He gave a short laugh at how far ahead of himself he was getting.

He might be tall enough to see into tomorrow, but he hadn't looked there in a long, long time.

He'd forgotten how bright it was.

So bright he could hardly stand it.

SEVEN DAYS later, Emily felt like she was living in a bubble, waiting for Win's punishment to end. She began to wonder if his father had grounded him for life.

Not that there wasn't plenty to distract her. Vance was suddenly on a home improvement kick, which was a good thing, except every morning Emily woke up to hammering on the roof, or the roar of a lawn mower in the backyard, or the sharp, pungent scent of house paint. When Emily asked Vance what was the hurry, he told her rain was coming and he wanted all the work done before then.

A heat wave had hit Mullaby that week, so Emily couldn't believe rain was coming any time soon. But every time she would come downstairs, irritable from the heat, Grandpa Vance would tell her not to worry, rain was coming to cool things off. When she finally asked him how he knew, he told her his elbow joints told him so. She didn't argue, because she really didn't want to get into why he was talking to his elbow joints.

Every day, when Vance took his afternoon nap, she would go next door just as an excuse to spend some time in an air-conditioned house. It didn't exactly work to her favor, though. Despite the heat, every day Julia made a cake with her kitchen window wide open. When Emily asked her why, she said she was calling to someone. Emily didn't question this. That Julia believed it was good enough for Emily. While Julia baked, Emily told her about Win, and Julia seemed glad that Emily now knew. Emily knew that Julia had forgiven her mother for what she'd done. Julia seemed to be doing a lot of forgiving lately. She'd lost a lot of her restlessness.

At five o'clock every day, Julia would leave with the cake she'd made, just as Stella came home from work. On the seventh day of this happening, Emily finally asked Stella where Julia was taking the cakes. At first she'd assumed she was taking the cakes to her restaurant, but she became curious when she realized Julia never returned in the evenings.

"She takes them to Sawyer," Stella said.

"Does he eat all that cake?" Emily asked.

"Don't worry. He burns it all off." Stella looked shocked at herself. "Erase that. You didn't hear that. Crap. I need a glass of wine. Remember, do as I say, not as I do."

Emily liked sitting on the back porch with Stella after Julia left, the slow pace of the day as it turned into evening, waiting to go eat dinner with her grandfather. Stella would sometimes talk about

272

Emily's mother. She was a champion storyteller and had a wild past, which was a great combination. Emily never sensed that Stella was anything but happy with her life as it was now. She got the feeling the stories were worth more than Stella's desire to go back and do anything differently.

As she headed back home that evening, she realized that, if possible, the heat made things in Mullaby move even slower. There were still plenty of tourists, but the neighborhoods were quiet, with only the occasional hum of a window fan or air conditioner gliding from houses as she passed them. It was as if everyone was in stasis, waiting for something to happen.

Finally, that night, it did.

A terrific thunderstorm erupted just as darkness fell. It came on so strong that Emily and Vance had to race around the house closing the windows. They laughed as they did so, making a game of it, then they stood on the front porch and watched the sheets of rain. The ending of that day felt like she was coming to the end of a story, and suddenly Emily felt sad. She made excuses to stay up with Grandpa Vance. They played cards and looked through photo albums Vance magically produced, full of photos of her mother.

Finally, Grandpa Vance said he was tired and she reluctantly said good night to him. She went upstairs and walked into her room, and realized that she'd forgotten to close her balcony doors.

Rain was flying in and the floor was soaked. She spent nearly an hour wiping down the floor, the doors, the walls, and all the nearby furniture. She dropped all the wet towels in the bathtub, then stripped out of her wet clothes.

She put on a cotton nightgown and fell into bed. The temperature had dropped sharply, and it felt almost decadent to cover herself with a sheet. The clatter of drops against the windows on the balcony doors sounded like raining coins.

A few hours later, she woke up as she was unconsciously kicking the sheet off. Everything was quiet, a strange sort of quiet that felt like an unfinished sentence. The storm had passed and it was uncomfortably hot in her room now.

She opened her eyes and saw that moonlight was now filtering in through the gaps in the curtains on the closed balcony doors. She slowly got out of bed and went to the doors to open them. The limbs of the trees were so heavy with rain-water that some of them almost touched the balcony floor. The heat of a typical Southern summer night was back, the humidity oppressive, but the moonlight reflecting on the wet surfaces made the neighborhood look like it was coated in ice.

All this had been so foreign at first. She hadn't known, when she'd first arrived, that she would grow to love this place like she did.

There were a lot of things she hadn't known when she'd first arrived.

Strange and wondrous things.

The light from the moon shone along the door casing and spread across the walls a few inches inside, far enough for her to suddenly notice that the phases-of-the-moon wallpaper she'd been living with all week was gone. It was a now curious dark color she couldn't quite make out, punctuated by long strips of yellow. It looked almost like dark doors and windows opening, letting in light. The wallpaper was usually some reflection of her mood or situation, but what did this mean? Some new door was opening? Something was being set free?

When she finally realized what it meant, she spun around, her eyes darting around the room until she found him.

Win was sitting on the couch opposite her bed. He was leaning forward, his elbows on his knees, his hands clasped.

"My punishment ended as of midnight," he said.

Her heart began to race. It was so good to see him. And yet, she felt unexpectedly awkward. "So . . . so you were just going to sit there until I woke up?"

"Yes." He stood. It made a swishing sound in the silence. He walked to the balcony doors. She was standing in a square of moonlight, and he stopped just short of it, like it was a line he couldn't cross.

"I'd almost forgotten what you looked like,"

she said, joking. A bad joke. Why was she so nervous?

Because he had almost kissed her.

"I spent all my time remembering what you looked like," he said seriously.

"I had people hammering and sawing and mowing all around me. It was hard to concentrate."

He gave her a funny look. "That's your excuse?"

"And there's no air-conditioning in this house. Do you know how hard it is to concentrate when you don't have air-conditioning?" She needed to stop, but couldn't seem to.

"Your grandfather had the largest limb of the oak that stretched to your balcony cut down. I had a hell of a time getting up here this time."

That finally drew her up short. She stared at him in the shadow. "How many times have you come up here?"

"A few."

She suddenly thought back to the day she'd arrived in Mullaby. "The day I arrived, my bracelet on the table . . ."

"I knew you were coming in that day," he said. "I was curious about you. I found the bracelet on the front walk."

"You don't have to sneak in here anymore," she said. "Everything's out in the open now, right?"

His answer was to step into the light in front of her, so close they almost touched.

Nothing happened at first. But then, like it was

growing so hot it became white, the glow around him started to blaze. She looked up at him and he was watching her closely.

"I lied," she whispered.

He looked concerned and started to step back. "About what?"

She reached out and stopped him. "About forgetting what you looked like. I could never forget this. I *will* never forget this," she said. "Not in all my life."

He smiled and took her face in his hands.

Then he finally kissed her.

Chapter 16

Maddie Davis adjusted the backpack on her shoulder as she walked down the side-walk. She'd arrived in Mullaby yesterday and was staying at the Inn on Main Street. Her parents had arranged it. She'd wanted to do this alone, but she understood that her parents were worried, and if paying for her stay at a swanky inn made them feel better, then she would suffer through it and diligently eat the chocolate put on her pillow every night.

She hadn't slept well the night before. The full moon had poured through the window in her room, and she'd spent most of the night curled up in a chair, staring at the park across the street from the inn. At breakfast, the innkeeper had told her that the full moon in August was called the Sturgeon Moon. It made people restless, she'd said, like there was too much to do, too many fish to catch.

After breakfast, Maddie had talked to her mom and had tried to keep it light. But her mother had still sounded nervous. "Maybe my sarcasm will finally be explained," Maddie had joked. "Maybe it's simply hardwired. That means it's not your fault." Her mother hadn't laughed. Maddie should have known. Her parents were the kindest people she knew, but they didn't share Maddie's sense of humor. She'd learned early on to temper her smart mouth around them.

It was a perfect, sunny Monday morning. As Maddie walked, she took a deep breath of the tangy-sweet air and her shoulders relaxed a little. She liked this town. It reminded her of something she couldn't quite place.

She saw the sign hanging over the door ahead. J'S BARBECUE.

For some reason, she stopped. Her feet simply wouldn't move. The people behind her had to break around her as they walked past.

She'd thought about doing this for years, and it was time. But she'd tried to downplay the seriousness of the event by blocking out only a few days to do it. She'd sandwiched it between the end of her summer internship at her father's law firm and her first day back at school at Georgetown for her sophomore year. But now that it was really going to happen, she wasn't sure she wanted to go through with it. What was it really going to accomplish? She had a great relationship with her adoptive parents. And she already knew enough about her birth mother to piece together why she'd given Maddie up for adoption. Julia Winterson had been sixteen and a student at Collier Reformatory, a now-defunct institution that had been groundbreaking at the time, a boarding school for troubled girls. It had closed down a few years ago because of budget cuts. Julia now lived in a small barbecue town in North Carolina and owned a restaurant. She'd never married. Never had more kids. The private investigator her parents had hired on Maddie's behalf had even supplied a photo of Julia. She was pretty and fresh, but with a faraway look in her dark eyes. Maddie, with her blond hair and blue eyes, didn't look much like her, except maybe a little around the mouth. She figured she must take after her birth father, whoever he was. His name wasn't on her birth certificate. That was one thing only Julia could tell her.

She started walking again, but her heart was racing. She could hear it in her ears. She was almost to the large front window of the restaurant when she stopped again, this time collapsing back against the brick façade of the building. She set her backpack by her feet and covered her eyes with the palms of her hands.

Don't be a wuss, she told herself.

She let her hands fall to her sides.

When she opened her eyes again, she saw that she was standing opposite two teenagers sitting on a bench outside the restaurant. The girl had quirky flyaway hair and was dressed in shorts and a tank top. The young man was in a white linen suit and red bow tie. They were leaning in toward each other, their foreheads almost touching, and the guy had the girl's hand in his, slowly rubbing his thumb over her wrist. They were in their own world. The prince and princess of their own kingdom. It made Maddie smile.

They both looked up when the door to the restaurant opened. Maddie turned her head, her eyes widening. The elderly man walking out had to duck under the doorway to get out. She'd never seen someone so tall.

The teenagers stood when they saw him. The giant walked over to them with an awkward, stiff-legged gait. The young man held out his hand and the giant shook it. They said a few words, laughed at something, then the guy in the white suit turned and walked down the sidewalk.

When he passed Maddie, he smiled slightly and gave her a polite nod. She watched him walk away, then turned back to the giant and the girl. The giant handed the girl a paper bag. She took it and together they walked down the sidewalk. Maddie craned her head to look up at him as he passed.

She felt like she was in some strange fairy tale, like she'd just dropped into the ending of a story.

The door to the restaurant opened again and two men walked out. Silver sparkles from inside caught in the air and rolled in the wind past her. She took a deep breath, and it made her stand up straighter. Sugar and vanilla and butter. That relentless scent had been following her around all her life. Sometimes she could see it, like this, but most of the time she just *felt* it. When she was a kid, she could be sitting in class at school, or walking her dog Chester, or in the middle of a dreary violin lesson with her older brother, and the smell would suddenly appear out of nowhere and make her inexplicably restless. Even now, sometimes she would wake up at night and swear someone was baking a cake in the house. Her roommates thought she was crazy.

It was the familiarity of the smell that gave her the courage to pick up her backpack and walk to the window and look inside the restaurant. It was a plain, nondescript place, but packed.

Maddie's eyes went to a woman behind the counter right away. There she was.

Julia Winterson.

The woman who'd given birth to her.

She was smiling, talking to a handsome man with blond hair sitting on the other side of the counter. Maddie had spent countless hours staring at the photograph from the private investigator.

In real life Julia looked happier, more settled.

Maddie kept her eyes on her through the window as she slowly walked to the door. When she reached the door, she saw that there was a flyer taped to it that read:

Blue-Eyed Girl Cakes:
Specialty cakes for any occasion.
Inquire within.

Someone else walked out and, seeing her, held the door for her.

"Are you ready?" the man asked.

The ending of one story. The beginning of another.

"Yes. I'm ready," she said, then stepped inside.

A Year of Full Moons

The full moon in January: ***The Full Wolf Moon***
According to lore, under this moon, wolves would howl in hunger outside Native American villages. When the moon is full in January, people tend to eat too much, drink too much, and play too much trying to fill a winter emptiness.

The full moon in February: ***The Full Snow Moon***
February is traditionally when the heaviest snow falls. People often dream of places they'd rather be when they sleep under a full Snow Moon.

The full moon in March: ***The Full Worm Moon***
In the spring, the ground softens and earthworms reappear . . . as do the robins who eat them. The lure of possibly getting caught while doing something daring or scandalous is hard to resist during the first full moon in March.

The full moon in April: ***The Full Pink Moon***
This full moon marks the appearance of pink ground phlox, an early spring flower. The amount of hope in the air during a full Pink Moon makes it the best time to ask someone to marry you.

The full moon in May: ***The Full Milk Moon***
The abundance of greenery to eat at this time of year gives cows and goats the potential to produce rich, fortified milk. People often think they are the most attractive under a full Milk Moon.

The full moon in June: ***The Full Strawberry Moon***
June is typically when strawberries ripen and are gathered. The best time to seek forgiveness is under the Strawberry Moon. Sweetness seems to linger during this time.

The full moon in July: ***The Full Buck Moon***
Bucks begin to grow new antlers at this time. Young men will butt heads and generally show themselves under this full July moon.

The full moon in August: ***The Full Sturgeon Moon***
Native American lore says that the sturgeon of the Great Lakes and Lake Champlain were most easily caught during the full moon in August. This full moon tends to make people feel restless and overwhelmed.

The full moon in September: ***The Harvest Moon***
This is the full moon nearest the autumnal equinox, bright enough to allow farmers to work late into the night, bringing in the last of their harvest. A time of introspection. People are often moody during this moon.

The full moon in October: ***The Full Hunters' Moon***
Historically, after the harvest, with leaves falling and fields bare, it was easier to see to hunt under this full moon. If you stare at a Hunters' Moon with a question, it will become clear what has to be done.

The full moon in November: ***The Full Beaver Moon***
Beaver traps were set during this time, before the waters froze, so furs would be in abundance for the cold months ahead. For some people, the full Beaver Moon is the last chance to do something they've wanted to do but put off, before the heaviness of winter settles over them.

The full moon in December: ***The Full Cold Moon***
The full moon heralding long, dark, cold nights ahead. Unquestionably the best sleeping moon of the year.

Acknowledgments

As always, my undying gratitude to my family and friends for their love, support, and patience. I'll stop talking about barbecue now. I promise. And special thanks to Andrea Cirillo, Kelly Harms Wimmer, Shauna Summers, and Nita Taublib. This book would not have been possible without your input. I'd give you the moon, but you already gave it to me.

About the Author

SARAH ADDISON ALLEN is the *New York Times* bestselling author of *Garden Spells* and *The Sugar Queen*. She was born and raised in Asheville, North Carolina, where she is currently at work on her next novel. To learn more about Allen, visit her website at www.sarahaddisonallen.com.

Center Point Publishing
600 Brooks Road • PO Box 1
Thorndike ME 04986-0001 USA

(207) 568-3717

US & Canada:
1 800 929-9108
www.centerpointlargeprint.com